Inn Between Worlds

Volume 1

-Edited by-

Thomas A Farmer

ISBN-13: 978-0-9987679-0-1

ISBN-10: 0-9987679-0-5

Published by: Black Knight Books, 2017

Table of Contents

Gideon Wallace

-and-

The Sapphire Woman

-by-

Thomas A Farmer

Like many things, this is for my wife, Stephanie,
who also came up with the title.

The planet was called Pelleus IV, and in another life, it had been going to be a barren hunk of ice in seven thousand years. Now, green fields stretched away to Gideon's left and crashing waves to his right. Away from the shore, the land dropped away precipitously, and a cool breeze blew in across deep, indigo chop. With it came the smells of salt and ocean that reminded him of the London home he left on the other side of existence.

Gideon's current visit was superfluous. He finished the real work a hundred and ninety centuries ago, but the draw of the planet—the draw of being the first human being to set foot on its living soil—proved impossible to resist. Despite that, if Gideon was being completely honest with himself, this particular job had been one of his more boring and routine assignments. A few button presses and he was done.

Still, he felt a touch of empathy with the planet he helped save from death. In another life, Pelleus IV would have drifted into the path of a massive comet that would have pulverized its crust. Victim of a freak accident, the planet would have burned to a cinder as bits of rock and metal would have been ripped away by the impact. Worse, because the comet struck the planet on the outward leg of its orbit, Pelleus IV would have been pushed out of the so-called "Goldilocks Zone." In that reality, the fires gave way to ice within a hundred generations.

Debris rings from the impact would have settled into a regular pattern a few thousand years from his current time. Gorgeous, though short lived, they posed a serious problem for the colonists aboard the *Staraveth*, who originally emerged from cryogenic stasis to find their paradise of a destination reduced to a cold hulk.

Apparently, the disaster also opened a portal at the impact site. Five hundred years after the *Staraveth* arrived at the cold corpse of Pelleus IV, a man named Kennedy stumbled through the portal, found Gideon, and pleaded his case.

Now, two thousand years after starting work on a job given to him by a man who would not be born for another seven millennia, Gideon felt justified in taking the weekend to admire his handiwork.

Admittedly, his handiwork had been a very small part of the whole. He organized the project, but the actual heavy lifting had been carried out by a creature that insisted its name was Pavarotti.

Introduced to Gideon by a mutual friend, Pavarotti turned out to be a seven-kilometer spacefaring leviathan with an odd fascination for opera. Regardless of its musical tastes, Pavarotti had been the key player in maneuvering several asteroids into positions that altered the course of the planetkiller that would have been going to hit Pelleus IV in just a few minutes.

The plan worked, as originally evidenced by a visit from a much healthier, and much more confused, Kennedy who came to tell Gideon the news. Gideon smiled at that particular memory— apparently leaving a message carved in the stone of a cave addressing the man by name had produced something of a stir.

The portal appeared on Pelleus IV's moon for that version of Kennedy, a fact which Gideon found somewhat surprising. To be fair, Gideon found it surprising that Pelleus IV had a moon at all. When he, Pavarotti, and the rest of the project crew first came to the planet two thousand years before, the skies had been empty of any lunar objects.

He was not going to complain. When their part of the project began, the portal from the asteroid impact had not yet formed. At that point, the portal waited a kilometer out to sea, seven meters below the surface. As surprises went, spending two full minutes under deep water at night—because of course the relative time shift dumped him out at three a.m.—was not one he wanted to repeat. In his corduroy coat, pockets laden with gear, simply judging the direction of gravity had been a challenge. Eventually, he risked the last of his air to form a stream of bubbles and followed them to the surface.

Worse, however, his old hat lay at the bottom of the planet's ocean, assuming it had not been consumed by some sea bass analogue on the way down

Gideon smiled again. He supposed he had become a bit jaded if nearly drowning while hopping through time to alter the course of a ten-kilometer asteroid with the help of a living starship was on the "boring" end of things.

A few more minutes passed during which Gideon continued to enjoy the simple, serene beauty of the planet. He had nowhere to be, but the rumbling of his stomach reminded him of the one shortcoming of his current location. If the *Staraveth* was not going to arrive for another seven thousand years, dinner was going to be a very long way off.

He checked his watch. Disguised as a simple brass pocket watch, the device also functioned as a highly detailed scanner for his surroundings. At the moment, what he wanted was exactly what it looked like the watch provided: the time.

Gideon told himself he would wait a few more minutes before leaving. Opening a portal now meant he would miss a spectacle two thousand years in the making. Still, with nothing to do until then, he withdrew his small portal controller from the thigh pocket of his topcoat. Taking a moment now to set the coordinates on the little tablet would save time later. Plus, Gideon learned early on never to leave his destination up to the moments

4

right before opening a portal. Rushing in instances like that was a gamble, at best.

He could have used the natural portals, relying on his own tech to do little more than stabilize them. But with one portal under the sea and the other on the moon that apparently existed now, creating his own was much more convenient. He was just glad Allotech refined their designs to the point where the process no longer drew the attention of the star gods. *That* was an ordeal Gideon would never consider boring.

As he fiddled with the controller, the wind kicked up, taking away Gideon's hat—the one which replaced the hat now at the bottom of the sea. The felt tophat swirled away on the sudden gust, floating a dozen meters inland. He cursed, dropped the controller back into his pocket and turned to retrieve the wayward piece of clothing.

Halfway to it, the wind swirled again, picking the lightweight hat up and throwing it another few meters. This time it stayed put, and Gideon retrieved it with minimal effort. With an exaggerated frown, he dusted it off and placed it firmly back onto his head.

The hand that reached a second time for his pocket watch stopped halfway there as the sound of feet crunching on gravel some distance away took the entirety of his attention.

Several thoughts went through Gideon's mind right then, but the foremost of them was that no one, other than perhaps Pavarotti, knew he was here. Pavarotti would not make footstep sounds, so that ruled out the possibility of the living starship having come to pay an unexpected visit.

Rather than retrieve his watch, he dropped his hand to the holster hanging from his belt. All in one go, Gideon

5

accomplished three things. First, he pivoted on his heels to face the source of the sound. Second, his left hand extended to ward off any blows coming in from short range. Third and finally, he drew and leveled his revolver.

A younger Gideon would have drawn a knife, but that younger Gideon did not have a proper respect for the ways in which someone could do him harm at a distance. His pistol might have *looked* like a LeMat revolver straight out of his parents' generation, but the shell was an aesthetic choice that disguised the gun's advanced inner workings. Instead of bullets, each one of the revolver's nine cylinders held a different, and complete, weapon.

His thumb cocked back the hammer to arm the default cylinder, a simple stunner. He leveled the pistol, then immediately relaxed. The man standing a few meters away was no stranger and certainly no assassin. Like Gideon's Nineteenth Century wardrobe, the other man's polished breastplate and Conquistador sword belied incredibly advanced technology. The rainbow plume of ostrich feathers protruding from his helmet, on the other hand, were nothing but decoration.

"Come now, Gideon. You wouldn't shoot your old partner, would you?"

Gideon gently lowered the hammer on his pistol, pointing it at the sky just in case, and grinned. "Certainly not in the face, Senhor Santiago. Perhaps in the thigh for sneaking up on me."

"Then I would be forced to see a machinist and acquire an entirely new leg. That would hardly be fair."

"You could stand for an upgrade."

"I couldn't stand without an upgrade if you shot me, that's for sure!"

6

Gideon laughed. "A fair point."

"Plus," the erstwhile Conquistador continued, "I would send you the bill."

"That, my friend, would be cruel."

"Then I advise you to restrain your desire to poke holes in my limbs."

"Point taken. What brings you here, Ruben? Better, how did you find me?"

"When was easy. This evening was the original date for the asteroid impact. Where, well..." Ruben laughed and indicated the seascape with a dramatic flourish of his hand. Silk embroidery, or something that looked very much like it, fluttered at his wrist as it caught the sunlight. He smiled. "It took a bit of searching, but when you're the only other human on the planet, the search is a little easier."

"Stealth tech," Gideon replied. "I must invest in stealth tech."

"You'll never hide in an orange coat and a tophat."

"I'm not taking stealth advice from a Portuguese who considers polishing his armor a fun leisure activity."

Ruben's grin widened into a flash of teeth and twinned moustachio curls, and he took a bow. "Ruben Santiago does not need to hide!"

"That's quite a boisterous way to explain that you don't know how."

"One needn't learn stealth if one isn't a frail Englishman, Gideon."

"You wound my pride, Portuguese."

"I cannot help it, my friend. The larger targets are easier to hit."

Gideon mimed a wound in his chest, grabbing at the jacket over his heart. "Another deadly blow. And, I might add, a distraction."

Ruben raised an eyebrow. "From?"

"You haven't yet told me why you came in the first place."

"I can't pay you a visit to help commemorate your success?"

Gideon chuckled. "If you did, it would be the first time."

Now it was Ruben's turn to laugh again. "Not true. Did I not attend the celebration at Sunkiss?"

Gideon held up his hands in defeat. "Alright," he said, "once."

"At least. I'll make a list and bring it to you later."

"You do that."

Ruben finally approached the rest of the way and clapped Gideon on the shoulder. That close, it was clear how much larger the Kelt—Gideon only called him Portuguese to needle the man—actually was. Gideon had been on the lower end of things physically on his own Earth and Ruben Santiago came from a world where the Roman Empire never rose and the children of the *Keltoi* ruled.

Gideon supposed there were worse heights to reach than the Kelt's lace-wrapped throat.

Heavily spiced tobacco smoke lingered on his clothes and breath as Ruben spoke. "Truthfully, Gideon, I didn't come with good news, at least I think it's not good."

Craning his neck upward, Gideon asked, "you think?"

Ruben shrugged and stepped back to a more comfortable

distance. "There's a woman asking after you, my friend. I don't think she means you harm directly, but there's something off about her."

"Off?" Gideon chuckled. "Ruben, you've got to stop being so vague."

"Remember when we met the original CEO of Allotech?"

"Corinthus?"

Ruben nodded and Gideon shivered. Corinthus might have looked human, but something in his eyes said otherwise. The green glow had been bad enough, but Gideon knew enough about technology, even then, to know effects like that would be easy enough to replicate. No, something inhuman lurked behind his eyes, revealed in the moments before the portal cascade tore his planet apart.

"Don't tell me he's back."

"He's not."

Gideon let out a breath he had not been aware he was holding and tension left his shoulders. "You were saying?"

Ruben shrugged. "She felt like he did, only," the Kelt waved a hand at the ocean, "not. Corinthus felt evil, do you remember?"

Gideon did not, but that was hardly surprising. He could read people, their motivations and goals, easily enough. Years of business taught him that skill, but to grasp the somewhat more nebulous concepts of "good" and "evil" by feel was a talent he lacked.

Nonetheless, he nodded. Digressing down that road would not do them any good. It was hard enough to keep Ruben on a single story at a time without adding something to distract him.

The Kelt went on. "She did not feel evil. But, Gideon? That

9

same electric hum followed her around."

"Corinthus is dead," Gideon replied. "You don't think she was an ally of his?"

Ruben shook his head. "Doubtful. Again, she didn't feel evil like he did. Proud, sure, but Corinthus felt cruel. You remember, yes?"

That impression, Gideon did remember. Even before realizing he was not human, Gideon's business acumen picked out Corinthus's willingness to use people like tools. "Did she say what she wanted?"

Again, he shook his head. "No, only that she was interested in meeting you and had been asking around the Inn for a day or so before I arrived."

"Days by whose clock?" Gideon asked, giving voice to a question that would not have made any sense in any other context.

"At the Inn itself."

Gideon hummed. Time inside the Inn flowed at a constant rate, which meant very little for the multiverse outside it. Still, it provided the most reliable clock in all existence. More to the point, if this woman had been there for over a day, it would be rude to keep her waiting any longer. "I suppose my vacation here has taken long enough. Did you bring a controller?"

"I did," Ruben replied, then grinned. "How else would I have gotten here?"

"I would not put it past you to arrive in the middle of the ocean just to prove a point."

Ruben's smile widened again and he laughed. "Perhaps, but not today. At any rate, I'm not headed back there for a while. I

10

took a job myself just this morning. Well, another job."

"Something exciting, I hope?"

Now Ruben's face made the transition from "smile" to "excited grin." He took a step back so that he could gesture more fully with his arms. "Seven put out a call for soldiers yesterday. In fact, I was already on my way out when this woman found me and asked after you.

"'I'll find him,' I told her. She seemed most relieved to hear that. 'He'll be back eventually,' I said, but she was pretty insistent that she speak to you soon. 'Time is of the essence,' she said to me."

"And she couldn't come find me here?" Gideon asked.

Ruben shrugged. "You'll have to ask her yourself, Gideon. She didn't tell me much."

"Did 'she' have a name?"

Again, a noncommittal shrug. "That was one of the things she did not tell me. I am unsure how time could be 'of the essence' when we were talking to one another in the Inn, but that was how she phrased it."

Gideon chuckled, trying to butt into the story before Ruben could drift further from what Gideon would consider useful information. "Well," he said, then cleared his throat for emphasis. "Thank you for bringing me the news. As I said, I can cut this vacation short. I have the time, after all."

Ruben laughed. "Don't we all. Now, if you will excuse me, I must meet Sid before we deploy."

"Wait, Sid Belmonte? He took the job with you?"

Ruben beamed. "He was the one who brought me the listing, in fact. Apparently Seven reached out to him personally, and..."

"Ruben."

"...asked him to put together a team. Seven heard how we worked together against Corinthus and..."

"Ruben!"

"Yes?"

Gideon laughed. "Tell Sid I said hello, alright?"

The Kelt nodded, still grinning. "Of course, Gideon."

Ruben turned to leave, withdrawing his own portal control device from a pocket hidden inside his breastplate. A holographic interface sprang into life above the watch-sized lump of brass. Ruben's fingers manipulated ethereal menus and a point of white light appeared a meter and a half in front of his face.

The brilliant sparkle extended itself into a line that stopped a few centimeters above the ground. It hovered like that for a moment before swirling and twisting, impossibly thin and yet substantial enough that Gideon swore he could have measured its width with calipers. How something without a third or even second dimension could twist was lost on Gideon's brain, but his eyes insisted the line twisted and curled around itself before spreading out and forming a rectangle just a little bigger than a door.

Gideon's eyes could not focus on the perfectly black surface of the portal. "Surface" was a misnomer for something that, like the line it sprang from, had no third dimension, but it looked solid enough to stop bullets right up until the moment that Ruben stepped through and into infinite blackness.

The Kelt and his gleaming armor disappeared and the black rectangle shrank back into a line which collapsed further into a point of light before winking out of existence altogether. In moments, all that was left to show Ruben Santiago ever existed were his footprints and the lingering hint of tobacco smoke on the air.

Gideon, for the third time now, withdrew his portal controller. With his other hand, he checked his watch again.

"Thirty seconds," he said, using that time to double-check the portal coordinates. Moving from universe to universe was easy compared to where he would be going after leaving the planet.

He craned his neck upward, using the moon that existed in this universe to gauge positions in the sky. It was too early for stars, but the planet's sun was low on the opposite horizon. The steel gray sky was clear, another reason Gideon selected this spot in particular.

Another few seconds passed and Gideon frowned. Either his calculations were off or the sky was still too bright and he would have to re-adjust his coordinates to do something drastic like watch the spectacle from the moon.

Fortunately, he did not have to do that. As it turned out, he was simply forty-three seconds early. The streak appeared in the eastern sky, opposite the sun, and gradually elongated until it stretched across the sky like a chalk tally mark.

The comet's progress across the sky was slow, something that would likely take the better part of a day to pass overhead. After wrapping around the sun's gravity and perturbed in its eons-old path by Pelleus IV and its new moon, the comet would return every three-hundred and eighty-one years. Now that it was not trying to kill every living thing around him, the sight was actually rather beautiful.

He raised a hand in mock salute. "Gideon Wallace: One. Planetkilling Comet: Zero."

With that last remark, he tapped the activation button on his portal controller. Like Ruben's portal, it sprang into existence a few paces away. Tracking a near infinite number of portals through time and space required more math than Gideon could hope to understand, but "zero" was easy enough. "Zero," in a multiverse with no center, was the place through which each of the portals passed on the way to its destination. Trying to go there, however, was a feat not unlike exiting a moving train safely at a stop with no platform.

Gideon's portals appeared oval-shaped, which he considered to be more aesthetically pleasing than a simple rectangular door. If anyone or anything else was going to interrupt him, the opportunity would only exist for another few seconds.

He took another deep breath, tasting the salt air from the sea, and bid Pelleus IV goodbye. Perhaps he would return in seventy or seventy-five centuries and see what the crew of the *Staraveth* did with the planet they asked him to save.

As he stepped toward the perfect blackness that his mind demanded be some sort of mirror, Gideon amended another thought to that chain.

"Zero" also meant home, the Inn Between Worlds.

***

Gideon returned to the Inn with a very specific plan in mind. He would go to his suite, leaving some of his equipment and probably his hat and coat there, and then go down to eat. Plans afterward depended on who, if anyone, he came across in the process. First, however, he had to find his suite.

The Inn mutated with every person who came through, and it did so differently for each of those potentially thousands of souls. For Gideon, the place between realities provided a suite that

14

existed only when he was present. Its interior never changed unless he changed it and everything left inside remained as he left it.

Friends told him the door remained even when he was absent, but it was locked and resisted every attempt to break in. Even tools which should have made short work of what appeared to be a simple wooden door failed to make a mark—unless, that is, Gideon was present, at which point his door was just like any other door in the Inn.

The transitions this time were even more jarring than usual. Gideon stepped into an anteroom pulled directly from soft science fiction. Random control panels dotted the oddly rounded walls as soft light emanated from strips of cool blue where crown molding should have been. Strangely comfortable J-shaped chairs sat momentarily unoccupied.

"This is new," he muttered. "Wonder who brought this in?"

From there, things transitioned to stone and then to wood as he wound his way through twisted corridors to his room. The paths might have been less twisted than some days, but the halls were nothing he could consider "straight" or even "easily navigated" today. He said his hellos to a few people as he passed, promising to return for dinner after dropping his things in his suite. None of them mentioned the woman from Ruben's story.

Today, his room was on the second floor of a wooden guild house. His door was unmistakable, second in a long line that stretched past the vanishing point and seemed to spiral around and upward—he saw no other staircase. It was certainly preferable to the half-mile hike through a limestone cavern that it had been before taking the job at Pelleus IV.

Inside, he automatically doffed his outerwear, throwing the

hat into the top shelf of his suite's living room armoire. The belt and gun holster went on a peg on the outside. He hung his coat and waistcoat just below the hat and shut the door, starting the machine's cleaning system. Like so much else in the Inn, his armoire looked ancient, but concealed an array of advanced technologies. It could be programmed to maintain any garment, or even simple tools, and Gideon stored most of his outerwear in its oak walls. For his tastes, it maintained the sort of slightly worn, lived-in look that he preferred, while still repairing any real damage.

It was then that Gideon noticed a new door in the living room. It occupied a stretch of wall previously covered by a painting of the sun silhouetting the largest of Sunkiss's floating mountains. His reading chair should have been a pace away, enough room to look up and appreciate the skyscape, but not so close that Gideon could knock into it if he moved the chair.

The painting had been shifted to one side to accommodate the new door and his reading chair now sat several paces away from the door, on the side opposite the painting.

Gideon frowned, withdrawing his LeMat from its holster, but leaving the belt hanging on the side of the armoire. Habitually, he checked the various mechanisms archaic and futuristic, then the new door. For the moment, it was locked and so left it where it was.

Technically, the Inn was a place where violence "did not happen." That technicality was enforced by the permanent inhabitants, himself included, and had nothing to do with the nature of the Inn itself. Gideon did not mind having neighbors, but the sudden appearance of a door in his formerly unchangeable suite set off a warning bell in his mind.

Carrying the gun into the bathroom, he mentally compiled a

list of things that needed to be done before dinner. Certain things were more important than finding out why there was a strange door in his suite and, despite two centuries to break the habits, he remained a product of nineteenth-century England.

With his pistol within easy reach, Gideon disrobed the rest of the way. Shirt and pants went into a separate cleaning machine, one that was less sophisticated than the armoire holding his coat and hat. With hands steadied by two hundred years of experience, Gideon prepped the shaving soap and razor, completing the process in just a few minutes.

Five more minutes resulted in a fresh shirt and pants, which Gideon laid out on his bed while rummaging around for the rest of the outfit. Even in the Inn, or perhaps especially here, presentation at dinner was important. Gideon pushed a line of hanging clothes aside, dissatisfied with all of them. Something motivated him to seek out something different, perhaps a brighter shade than his usual choices. He supposed it was Ruben's message; if he were to meet a potential new employer, Gideon supposed he should make an extra effort.

A flash of color at the back of the closet caught his eye and Gideon withdrew a brilliant, sapphire blue cravat. It had been a gift from a friend nearly a hundred years ago now and complemented the dark orange of his topcoat nicely, but Gideon considered it too bright for normal wear. Still, it seemed to call to him and he added it to the pile of clothes on the bed.

Last, to cover up the smells of work and salt from Pelleus IV, Gideon went back to the bathroom. In the cabinet above the sink waited various colognes and perfumes. Another few minutes worth of searching resulted in a bay rum based on a blend he created for himself two hundred years before, while working as a land broker in London. Splashing it on his neck resulted in a bloom of orange and rose. Under that lurked jasmine and juniper swirling in a deep base of dark vanilla.

Satisfied with that step, Gideon returned to the bed. Across the room, a setting sun that did not exist caught his eye. He went to the window, looking out over a dockside that also never, to his knowledge, existed. The ships out there had glittering holographic sails unlike anything his Earth ever produced. Of course, nothing was outside the Inn, not even "nothing." There simply was no "outside" at all, but the ocean view persisted nonetheless.

Watching as a submarine surfaced and unfurled a beautiful, glowing magenta sail that slowly pulled it across the harbor "toward" his window, Gideon went through the next steps of dressing for dinner. The last of those steps was to pierce the center of his sapphire cravat with a stud whose pea-size pearl had been taken from a clam about which "monstrous" did not even begin to suffice as a descriptor.

Like the harbor that was so similar to the view from his old office window, the bed where he laid out his clothes simultaneously reminded him of both of his old homes. In a different wood or another shade of stain, the features would have clashed with one another. The bed's four tall posts reminded him of the London where he had been born—dark, stolid, but hiding little minute details deep in the grain where most would never look. By contrast, the openwork headboard and footboard might have been called "art noveau" if they came from Earth, but they came from Sunkiss, an airy world of open skies, flying cities, and wingsuits. A world of bright sun, it had been his home before coming to the Inn, while first searching for Sid Belmonte and then while fighting Corinthus.

In the living room, his armoire complained with an indignant beeping noise when he opened the door early. The faint chemical odor from the inside dissipated in moments, and Gideon withdrew his coat first. Gideon bought it shortly before he accidentally left Earth the first time. Double breasted and cut with a tight waist like a frock, but with pockets and a belt, it was also one of the few items in Gideon's possession when he touched that first portal. The gun and its belt came later, and in a place like the Inn they served as a fashion statement as much as anything.

Gideon buttoned the coat, wrapped the gun belt around his waist, then spent a few moments adjusting bits of his outfit in the mirror until everything read with the proper air of casualness. The hat he transferred to a hatrack beside the suite's main door—the door that was supposed to be there. He was inside, after all, and wearing his hat indoors would not do.

He debated leaving the new door alone and going about his business as usual. After all, nothing here was permanent and it was bound to happen to his room sooner or later. Still, the mysterious door was exactly that: a mystery. If there was one thing Gideon could not resist, as evidenced by following what he thought was a will o' the wisp a very many years ago now, that thing was a mystery.

Going to the door, Gideon examined it in detail before even touching it. By appearance, it looked like any other wooden door. The surface was a little rough, perhaps, but the sort of roughness that came from years of things knocking into it rather than weather or deliberate damage. It had been revarnished at some point, and probably sanded and cleaned, but the character of the damage remained.

The brass doorknob was likewise subtly damaged and old. The rim had been polished smooth by a thousand-million hands, but the face bore scratches and marks of time. One large thumb-print, much larger than anything a human would have left, had been etched into the back of the knob, seemingly impervious to the wear of age.

He placed his hand on the doorknob, finding it on the cold side of things, but still a normal temperature. That, at least, was a good sign. Gideon had no desire to open a mysterious door and find it led to the center of a conflagration or the top of an ice mountain.

Taking another moment to tug fretfully at his tie and mouthing the words, "first impressions, Gideon," he wondered what might be waiting for him. Human was the most likely answer, but nonhuman species made up a full quarter of the Inn's population at any given time.

He knocked. "Hello?"

A moment passed before a female voice replied, "come in."

He hesitated a moment, a short one, before turning the knob and opening the brand-new, ancient door. The room on the other side was an artist's representation of what the London of his time might have looked like in a world where gears and mechanical iconography dominated. The usual things were present, but every last one of them had been styled to look far more complex than was necessary, the ultimate triumph of form over function.

A woman walked in from the other room dressed in a similar artist's rendition of the fashions of his mortal youth. Her clothes took even more liberties with history, or at least the history of his world, than her room did. A brownish gold skirt flowed from her waist, but only in the back. The front of her right leg was shrouded by what would have been part of a lace crinoline in his world, and aside from stocking and garter, her right leg was bare

20

nearly to the hip. A brocade corset, black velvet set against a very dark gray satin, topped that. It stopped just under her breasts, which were only partially covered by a silver blouse. Her shoulders and arms were covered by a bolero in a color just different enough from her skirt to be noticeable.

Her face, the last thing Gideon noticed as his eyes traveled around the artistically-interpreted room, was gorgeous in its own right and sported intense, dark makeup more akin to the Earth of two centuries after his birth than to anything truly Victorian.

If everything in front of him had been calculated to hold his attention, Gideon supposed this was the perfect way to do it. It all was just enough like what he grew accustomed to before falling through that first portal to project familiarity, but so very different in ways that grasped and held his attention.

She smiled, positively lighting up the room. Gideon felt irresistibly drawn to her for a moment, despite knowing nothing about her. Whatever else happened, he realized this was a person he needed to get to know, not just on an intimate level but on a practical one.

Gideon had spent nearly two centuries living in the Inn Between Worlds and in that time had developed a sense for when people were more than they appeared. Corinthus had given him that feeling, at least he had before Gideon, Reuben, Sid, and Helena trapped him in a special anomaly that—theoretically— erased his existence. Later, Umbras gave him the same impression, but that scar-faced man left before Gideon could do more than offer to buy him a drink.

Now, this woman gave off that same intangible aura of power. In reality, she could have been a talking rock and Gideon would have placed her firmly and instantly in his "get to know" list.

"Good evening," she said, striding across the room as though she owned it. She stopped a pace away from Gideon, just a little closer than he expected, and extended a hand. Gideon took it, finding her skin soft and warm, exactly as expected, but concealing a titanic strength that nothing about her silhouette indicated. "Catherine."

"Gideon Wallace," he replied automatically.

She nodded, still smiling, and stepped away. "I apologize for disrupting your room with," she waved in the direction of the doorway through which Gideon came, "that."

He shrugged. "It's nothing."

Catherine arched an eyebrow. "Really? I'm given to understand you're very particular about your neighbors."

"You've talked to the other guests, I see."

"Of course."

He cracked a grin. "The shastikan and I came to an understanding."

Again, she echoed his expression, grinning in response. Her face almost turned conspiratorial for a moment. "Actually, the story that came up the most was the weekend you shared a balcony with Sebastianus."

Gideon laughed. "Having to duel my way past him whenever we met, well, it got old. In my defense, there was a pool there the night before, and," Gideon emphasized the conjunction, "tossing him off the balcony meant he came to find me a few weeks later when he needed a hand on a mission. Wins all around."

"Stories abound, Gideon. You've been here for a while."

"Long enough," he admitted. "And you?"

"I come and go," she replied as a mysterious expression flickered across her face.

He took a half step backward to better size her up again. Now that he had a second look, Gideon chastised himself for not picking up on the obvious clues. She was not connected to power as he first thought. Rather, like Corinthus, she herself radiated power. Not only that, but she moved with a grace and ease which told him she knew how to use it.

He also picked up on the distinct feeling that she was not just watching him but silently examining him. Well, he thought with an inward groan as the cliché passed through his mind, two people could play at that game. Human or not—and if she was the same as Corinthus, whatever he was, then the odds leaned heavily toward "not"—some bits of body language were nearly universal. Even the giant living starship Pavarotti had body language that could be read from the right distance.

Subtle things about the way she moved backed up his initial impression. With every step, she remained perfectly balanced on her feet, ready and likely able to move quickly in any direction. Her eyes never remained fixed on one spot for more than a moment, but whenever they fell across him, Gideon felt like the intellect behind them laid him open to the soul.

Underneath it all was the same current of mental electricity he felt from Corinthus. The connection between her and the story-slash-warning from Ruben was obvious, but Gideon was not one to jump to conclusions. Rather, he preferred to skip briskly to conclusions one step at a time.

"May I sit?"

Catherine nodded, waving at hand in the direction of the richly decorated lounge area of her suite. Gideon dropped lightly onto a couch whose dark wood and royal purple accents spoke of England or France, but whose twisting, alien pattern never came from any Earth he knew. Still, eldritch and slightly four-dimensional as it was, the couch was certainly comfortable enough for his tastes.

"Tea?" Catherine asked.

"That would be lovely, thank you."

Gideon watched her leave, moving with the same grace she had shown since his arrival. When she returned mere moments later, she carried a gleaming silver tray with two small cups, an assortment of bowls, and a samovar. She placed it on the table in front of Gideon's seat, sitting herself opposite him and crossing her bare leg over the skirted one.

His attention fell on the samovar where it sat, all gleaming silver and enamel, in the middle of everything. The sides of the pot had been decorated in a stellar motif that reflected constellations he could not name. The top sported lettering the color of polished gunmetal, but only the first two faced him.

Gideon reached out and turned the pot toward him, revealing the entire word. "UMBRAS," it read in ornate, gothic blocks. Gideon carefully concealed his reaction, but felt sure that even the minute raise of his eyebrows did not escape Catherine's scrutiny. He stopped believing in coincidence three lifetimes ago, and Gideon knew for a fact that the scar-faced man calling himself Umbras did not loan his possessions to random rooms.

So, he thought, that was to be the game.

When he settled back into his seat, Gideon realized Catherine's brown eyes had fixed him with a deep intensity that was different from moments before. The first moments felt like a dissection, the same way Corinthus took apart his thoughts but less unpleasant. This was an evaluation.

He knew it showed on his face, but Gideon decided to leave the jump to that particular conclusion unsaid for the moment. He could mention it later, when it was appropriate. For the moment, there was tea to drink.

"Impressive workmanship," he quipped instead. "It's barely even warm on the outside."

"I assure you, Mister Wallace, the inside is much different from the exterior."

"There's not much here that you couldn't say that about."

"So I've noticed," she replied. Her lips quirked into a smile made all the more alluring by her nearly black lipstick. She shifted in place, putting both feet on the floor and leaning forward. "The tea should be ready. Shall I?"

He nodded. "Please." In his head, Gideon felt secure in the assumption that the tea inside that particular samovar had been ready since she brought it out. Whether she prepared it ahead of time or simply conjured it out of thin air, he could not say. In the Inn, either possibility could result in equally well-made drink.

Catherine turned the pot toward her, pulling the ornate UMBRAS out of his vision, and placed a cup under the spout. She twisted the knob and an aroma that all branches of humanity throughout time and space regarded as pleasant filled the air.

She filled the second before standing and crossing the small space to hand the cup to Gideon. Rather than return to her seat across the table, she sat instead in the chair immediately to Gideon's right.

He took a sip of the tea and, at least for a moment, all thoughts of the alluring woman in the next chair, along with the cloud of thoughts relating her to what Ruben told him earlier, vanished. A taste like woodsmoke filled his nostrils first, followed by saffron and rose intermingling. On their tails came bergamot and the unmistakable earthy anchor of the slow-roasted black tea itself.

"You approve?" Catherine asked, and Gideon was again aware that her dark eyes seemed to be judging everything he did.

He pointedly took another long sip, this time while keeping eye contact with her. That particular task proved harder than expected as her intense stare sent his heart racing, only not in the pleasant way he would have preferred.

Finally, Gideon did reply with a nod and a simple, "very much, yes."

She smiled. "Excellent."

Catherine took a long sip of her own tea before replacing the cup on the silver platter. Gideon did the same, draining his first. He sat back again, spreading his arms wide and draping one over the back of his chair. The shift in posture seemed to have its desired effect as Catherine's posture relaxed as well, though her maddeningly vague smile made it hard to pin down whether that change was deliberate or not.

"When did you arrive?" Gideon asked, then quickly added, "subjective time, of course."

"Of course." Her lips quirked into that smile again. "By the Inn's clock, early yesterday. I took the first empty room, which turned out to be already furnished, and styled my clothes to match. How convenient that it adjoined your own suite, Mister Wallace."

Convenient, yes, he thought. The Inn did not do 'convenient' things. Aloud: "call me Gideon."

26

Her smile brightened, becoming something truly mesmerizing for a moment. "Gideon, then."

Gideon reached for his cup with one hand, the samovar with the other. He turned it and worked the knob for a refill. Taking those few seconds to look closer at the designs on the side did not reveal any more useful information. If some message was hidden in those particular stars, it was lost on him.

Taking the cup in his hands, but not taking a drink, he said, "I have to admit, this is some of the best tea I've had in some time."

"Better than what they serve downstairs?"

He nodded, finally taking a drink of this second cup now that it had cooled some. The flavors were all still there, but this time his senses seized on the hints of rose. The bergamot and smoke faded into the background, replaced with a flavor that Gideon simultaneously swore was jasmine, and also swore had not been present in his last cup.

Gideon finished that cup in silence as Catherine refilled her own drink. A flash of curiosity passed over her features as she tasted the tea, but she said nothing even as her dark, analytical eyes found Gideon's again. That settled one mystery, he realized; the tea *was* changing flavor, and either Catherine had not expected that or the change in flavors somehow communicated something to her.

If not for the name at the top, he would have chalked that up to an ever-growing list of "mysteries of the Inn." Instead, it was time for another small conclusional leap.

With his empty hand, he pointed to the samovar. "That didn't come with the room, did it?"

She smiled. "No. It did not. It's mine, actually."

"Ah," he replied, trying to match her radiant smile with his own. "But it wasn't always?"

Catherine laughed, a sharp, sudden sound. "And he was worried you'd not remember him!"

Gideon chuckled. "Forget Umbras? How? If ever a human being could be called 'larger than life,' it's him."

"I'll be sure to never tell him that," Catherine said. "But yes, the entire set was a gift from the good General, oh, a thousand years ago now."

Gideon hummed. "So he *is* immortal, and," he paused, "General?"

"Oh, yes, General Umbras on the days he's feeling nostalgic for that particular part of his life. In fact, it was he who suggested I meet with you."

Gideon raised an eyebrow, hoping to conceal the fact that he nearly dropped his tea. He assumed Ruben Santiago told her about him and that his cryptic warning was the Kelt's idea of a mysterious reveal. If he knew Umbras was involved, Ruben's sudden desire to deploy on a mission, even one of Seven's Impossibilities, made a lot more sense.

Carefully, he set his tea down on the serving platter and folded his hands in front of his torso. "Well. You have my attention."

"I didn't before?"

"You have my *full* attention. Umbras doesn't so much as pick out his socks without a good reason, and if *he* told you to come find me, then I want to know why. Respectfully, I also want to know why *now* and dispense with further pleasantries."

Catherine smiled, a flash of enigmatic warmth. "Of course.

Tell me something, Gideon, do you remember a man named Vox?"

Gideon hoped the sudden chill he felt did not show on his face. There could be plenty of people in the multiverse named Vox. The vast majority of them were not white-haired, albino psychopaths with a fetish for chains. But if Umbras recommended him *specifically*...

He made himself nod. "Vox," Gideon said around a grimace. "The Lightning Reaper. Speaker for the Damned. He's a murderer, driven mad by amnesia and the ability to hear the laments of the dead. I thought him killed when Corinthus's planet was consumed by the Cascade."

Catherine frowned, a very obvious and not deliberate gesture. Not at Vox's name, Gideon realized, but at the mention of Corinthus. A shared history was obvious and later Gideon would have to ask about it. In the short term, he had a sudden rash of more immediate concerns.

Chief among them, as he said aloud, "but he didn't did he?"

"It would seem not."

"Alright," Gideon replied, then let out the rest of the air in his lungs. A deep breath later, he added, "if I may, I'm going to again cut to the chase. How long do I have? Why me? What are the stakes? Who can go with me? And what am I being paid?"

Catherine's demure smile returned and she held up a hand, ticking things off on her fingers as she replied. "First, very little time at all. Vox is now in the employ of another man like Corinthus, only perhaps worse because Taimethis believes that his goals are just."

Gideon snorted a laugh, remembering an aphorism which he paraphrased aloud. "Evil sleeps, but the tyranny of 'for your own

29

good' never rests."

"Precisely."

"That answers the next question, I think."

Catherine nodded. "Yes. For the third, I cannot say right now, other than to tell you that Taimethis is a very dangerous man and, while the stakes are not so high as they were against Corinthus, they are certainly of the same caliber."

Gideon fought to slow his racing heartbeat. Apocalyptic asteroids and murderous militias he could handle, but Corinthus violated the very laws of the universe themselves and brought down the wrath of the star gods.

His pay would have to be very high indeed.

"Next, I will go with you."

"You?"

She nodded. "I'm not surprised Umbras never mentioned me."

"Umbras didn't mention very many people."

Catherine frowned. "Yes, I imagine so. When you met him, some," she paused, "very bad things had happened to him."

"Your doing?"

Now, she turned that frown on him, and Gideon felt very small indeed. After a moment, it relented, and she said, "in part. Some time ago, I pushed him to take a deal that he did not fully understand."

Gideon arched an eyebrow. "That's not a good thing to admit when you're trying to get me to make a deal to fight against this Taimethis character."

"I can promise you," she said as a sudden wave of very obvious guilt washed over her. She repeated herself, "I can promise you that anything I tell you will be the truth and that I will tell you all I know as I learn it.

"That," she added, "is your pay."

His eyebrows went up. "'The truth' is my pay?"

"Haven't you ever wondered how this place works? Why it works?"

Gideon watched her for several seconds, frowning in thought. A great many things went through his mind, including the fact that he had only defeated Corinthus with the help of Ruben, Sid, John, Salazar, Helena, and a very lucky encounter with an angry star god. Still, if she was the same sort of being as Corinthus and Taimethis, and willing to help, that would do a lot to turn the tide of the fight.

Those concerns were irrelevant, however, as it seemed Catherine had done her proverbial homework after all and again presented Gideon the one thing he could not resist.

He sat back in his chair. "When do we leave?"

Catherine stood and offered her hand. "After dinner. Come."

Gideon stood and offered his arm. Catherine laid her hand in the crook of his elbow and again Gideon felt the impossible strength in her grip. Finding out what she was, whatever Corinthus and Taimethis were, might just be worth the danger he knew she was about to drop him into.

Gideon laughed, eliciting an inquisitive glance from Catherine, but said nothing. If danger could outweigh his sense of curiosity, he never would have touched that mysterious light all those years ago.

On the way out, Gideon surveyed her room in more detail. She claimed it was one assigned by the Inn, but now he seriously doubted that. Likely, as she was what Corinthus had been, even Gideon did not know what power she might have over the Inn. Her door shut automatically, and he spared an amused smile. Her choice of attire and décor, then, were appropriate. "Steampunk," as it was called, was just enough like the aesthetic of his home time, but different in enough ways, that in a moment's observation, Catherine encapsulated everything about his experience traveling through the Inn.

They stopped a moment at Gideon's room to allow him to lock the door, a process he relished given that his was one of the few permanent installations. Because of that permanence, having a locked door actually did something. He also retrieved his hat, tucking it under one arm.

The wooden walls on Gideon's floor told a story of ages long past. Running his fingers along the surface, he felt not the marks of a saw, but those of axes.

"Catherine," he said, "tell me something. An advance, if you will."

Beside him, she turned a quizzical eyebrow in his direction. She held that expression just long enough to elicit a nervous twitch at the corner of Gideon's own eye, then nodded. "What do you want to know?"

He stopped and again ran his fingers across the ax-hewn walls. "This. I've seen enough to know that 'real' can be subjective, but, is it real?"

Catherine laughed softly. "I'm going to need you to define real first."

"I was afraid you'd say that."

"I can tell you that this place is 'real' in the literal sense of the word. Your surroundings are made of matter."

"That's something. I'd hate to hallucinate something so," he eyed her and a smile cross his lips, "magnificent. But I meant," now Gideon touched a rough spot on the wall, or what looked like a rough spot. In reality, it was even smoother than the rest of the surface. "Did this wall ever exist somewhere else?"

Catherine's eyes twinkled and the corners of her mouth turned upward with what Gideon swore had to be amusement. "That's the right sort of question, my friend."

With his hand still on the wall, Gideon traced out the line where an ax had cut into it deeper than the other markings. He squinted, bringing his face level with the wounded wood. The cut ran deep, possibly all the way through the piece of wood, but was mostly filled in with something he assumed to be clay.

Gideon did not ever recall examining anything in the Inn so closely, but now that he was doing so, he found endless little details he might have walked past in anyone else's company. Catherine was fascinating, but in a way that turned his attention outward, not inward.

She joined him a moment later, touching the plank with the ax scar. "This piece came from a post-Viking people who called themselves Hälsafolk. In their world, Christendom never took hold in what you would call Europe."

"Sounds like Ruben's world," Gideon mused aloud.

Catherine nodded. "Similar circumstances, but when the *vikingar* of this world swept through, they stayed. This board," Gideon only now noticed a faint vibration in the wood, gone if he took his hand away, and only just barely perceptible otherwise, "came from a longhouse that was attacked in the night. A storm came and washed the invaders away, but not before lightning struck the hall."

33

"And this piece?"

"Gone," Catherine said, with a curious sadness.

Gideon raised an eyebrow. "Gone?"

"Surely you're not going to tell me that things do not simply disappear from time to time."

"I would have said that once," he admitted, then stopped. "Before."

"This board," she moved her hand one plank lower, "came from the interior wall of a ship sunk in battle against what you might recognize as the Spanish during the Battle of Cartagena."

"We had that in my world," Gideon said.

"Yes." Catherine smiled mischievously. "But did your version include the unexpected arrival of a well-outfitted Colonial Navy sailing from an America whose good welfare ensured constant allegiance to the Crown?"

"It did not," Gideon replied. He laughed, then suddenly sobered. "Do each one of these pieces have a story like that?"

"Everything and everyone here has been Lost." Something in her voice made the capital letter on "Lost" very clear to Gideon's mind. Before he could say anything however, she continued, "there's a candlestick downstairs, visually identical to twenty-two others, that fell from Odysseus's boat as it fell into the maw of Charybdis."

"Charybdis was just a whirlpool."

Again she flashed a mysterious smile. "In *your* world, perhaps."

"At any rate," Gideon said, straightening. "You mentioned dinner and, despite all else, I remain a slave to food."

"Of course."

Arm-in-arm, they descended to what today was the main floor. Axe-hewn wood gave way to marble walls and slate flagstones. The rooms all occupied the level above, and possibly the one above that. Gideon glanced upward and for a moment saw floor upon floor stacked so high that his mind started to swim with the immensity of it all, then a ceiling abruptly fixed itself three floors up.

The floor where they now stood appeared to have been taken from some sort of castle or palace. It felt neither old nor martial enough to be one of the old fortresses dotting the English landscape. But neither did it seem new enough to qualify for the term "palace" instead. He considered asking about it, but did not.

Signs that transformed themselves into English when he looked at them listed off various facilities, including an indoor pool that only appeared when a siren-like alien named Helth—or Gelth, Gideon never could master the peculiar consonant in mer name—visited. A moment's sweep across the spacious room told him in which direction the dining hall had relocated, and they went that way.

Two steps into the dining hall, which today had a bizarrely crystalline feel to it, he heard someone with a thick Mediterranean accent calling his name.

"Gideon!" the man called again, allowing him to pinpoint the location of the call.

Gideon's face broke into a grin and he raised the hand not currently wrapped around Catherine's elbow. He waved. "Leonidas!"

At his side, Catherine stiffened for a moment. Unlike her earlier reactions, this one was natural. Her attempt to control it took less than a heartbeat and if Gideon had not been touching her when it happened, he knew he never would have noticed.

"Come," he said. "Let me introduce you to my friend."

"Perhaps we should not."

"Nonsense," he replied. "I've known Leonidas for years now. It won't delay dinner more than a minute and," Gideon laughed, "if Sam's working this evening, it won't delay dinner at all."

Catherine tagged along, lingering a half step behind Gideon the entire way. She was not hiding, per se, but clearly continued to think that approaching Leonidas was a bad idea. She kept her hand in the crook of his elbow and did not attempt to lead Gideon in any other direction, however.

As he drew closer, Gideon noticed that between Leonidas and his tablemate, they had consumed a great deal of food and drink and seemed to be working their way through still more. The Spartan's personal clock was dramatically different from Gideon's. For him, it was likely very early morning. He suspected Leonidas had taken a contract and had woken up early that morning to engage in the same ritual in which he took part before every mission since the slaughter at Thermopylae—eat well, for tonight he might be dining in hell.

Leonidas's beard and hair had been freshly oiled, but the tunic he wore looked like any other. Gideon supposed the short, stocky man would be changing into his armor later. Like Ruben, and like Gideon himself, Leonidas preferred weaponry that felt like the things he was born with, despite their enhancements.

His tablemate had a similar air of aristocracy about him, but the other man was clad in only a red cloak and what appeared to be leather briefs. His hairless musculature could not have been sustainable with natural human metabolism, which might have explained the massive stack of plates and mugs next to him.

Leonidas stood up and wiped grease on the hem of his tunic. He extended a hand to Gideon, smiling, then his eyes slid to the side and went wide. He dropped to one knee with his hands clenched into fists and placed on the floor.

"Forgive me, my lady. I did not recognize you."

"Rise, King of Sparta," Catherine said.

Leonidas did so, his back ramrod straight.

"Relax," Catherine said, smiling. She touched Leonidas and he jumped in a way Gideon had never seen.

He took a breath, seeming to force the tension out of his muscles. Another breath and he looked at Gideon again, and again raised his hand to shake. When Gideon took it, Leonidas said, "I apologize. It's simply that I wasn't expecting your," his eyes slid sideways again, "companion."

Gideon filed that away in the list of things to ask about later. Aloud, he said, "it's alright. We were just coming down for dinner before heading out. Who's your friend?"

Leonidas laughed and motioned for his tablemate to stand. "Gideon Wallace, allow me, Leonidas of Sparta to present my newest acquaintance." His grin widened. "Leonidas of Sparta."

The other Leonidas towered over the one Gideon knew, standing just under Reuben Santiago's height. He extended a hand and, in an accent that was decidedly not Greek, said, "a pleasure to meet you, Gideon."

"You as well," he replied, then with a laugh, "Leonidas."

"Yes, it seems he and I are one and the same man but from very different worlds." The big man turned to Catherine and extended a hand. She took it and he bent low to kiss it. "A pleasure, indeed."

After the larger Leonidas sat down, Gideon turned back to the one he knew and said, "I won't keep you. Good luck out there, today."

"You as well," Leonidas replied. Again, he gave Catherine a momentary side-eye. "I fear you'll need it."

They stepped away from the Greeks, but before they were out of earshot, and thus at a distance where Gideon would have asked his question, he caught Leonidas's voice as he raised it for emphasis.

"Gideon... this morning... with Artemis!"

Gideon became aware of the sudden hitch in his step about the time Catherine's iron grip caught and steadied him.

"Artemis?" he asked.

The demure smile was almost frustrating in its mystery this time. "Many people have many names, Gideon."

"Yes, but that was Leonidas, man from a time when..."

The rest of his explanation was cut short by a portal opening in the middle of the dining room. While it was possible, it was bad form. The Inn had doors for a reason, everyone who came through more than once knew that. Even Gideon's portal generator emptied out into a void on the opposite side of whatever the Inn decided was its front door at that moment.

Opening a portal in the middle of the *dining room* was just rude.

A figure in black armor stepped through. Instead of a face, a visor, or something that might have been considered appropriate for the facial region, the newcomer simply presented a convex black mesh of metal.

He raised an armored blue glove, the only color on the entire outfit, and extended a finger. The other hand held a wickedly curved sword whose blade was as matte black as his armor. "Are you Gideon Wallace?"

Gideon's hand instinctively went for his gun. Leveling it, he replied, "I am."

"Come with me," the armored figure said. "We have located Vox."

Gideon cursed silently. To Catherine he said, "it would seem our dinner date has been interrupted."

"Perhaps not." She pointed to the table nearest the portal where a young man was leaving two metallic lunchboxes, clearly labeled with their names.

Gideon snatched up the box with his name on it. From the heft, it was either full, armored, or both. "Thanks, Sam." He looked around, but the Innkeeper was nowhere in sight.

"How does he do it?" he mumbled. Louder, "Catherine? Is he one of yours?"

"Perhaps," she said, "but most likely he works for our mutual friend, the General."

With faux hurt, he asked, "I'm not the only one you have looking for Vox?"

"Time is short," rumbled the hulking, armored figure.

Catherine smiled at Gideon. "You're not, no. You're just the only one looking for *Taimethis*."

"Well," he gestured to the sabre-armed man. "Lead the way."

***

Gideon emerged into a war-zone. It reminded him of his first

39

meeting with Sid; the feeling of that dense, dark forest was impossible to forget. The darkness punched through with sparks of lights, the shouts of anger and pain, and death on the chill winds all felt the same.

Through it all, shrill and piercing not because of the sound itself but because Gideon knew what was on the other end, chains clattered and creaked. Vox liked darkness; it had no effect on the blind man's ability to fight and kill. The hulking soldier, his work done, disappeared into the darkness in seconds. As he moved, twirling the black saber around himself like a protective wind of steel, only the blue of his gloves remained visible.

Gun in hand, Gideon pivoted on his heels to follow the figure into the smothering darkness. He could hear the chains as they moved, cracking and snapping through the air. When he went to bed the night before, Gideon was sure Vox was gone forever—erased from time, ripped apart at the molecular level, or whatever happened to matter caught in Corinthus's portal cascade.

With preparation, he might have changed out some of the elements in his gun. Against an enemy like Vox, Gideon had little need for non-lethal options, especially any that would disorient his target. On the other hand, the focused-gravity cannon masquerading as a twenty-gauge shotgun barrel would come in handy provided he could get a bead on Vox long enough to...

Catherine's iron grip interrupted his thoughts and Gideon realized he had only gone a few paces since exiting the portal. It shimmered behind him still, impossible blackness wreathed in colors the human eye was not meant to process.

"No," she said. Her voice held every ounce of iron that he felt in her grip and Gideon felt his feet root to that spot. Something more than strength was at work in her hand now. He had felt strong holds, even strength that other universes would have called

40

"heroic" or "superhuman," but Catherine was something different. Muscular power did not hold him in place, rather it was as though motion itself became impossible the moment she touched him.

The hold permitted him to turn, however, and he pivoted to face her. "No?"

"Like I said, we've got other work to do."

"I've fought Vox before."

"Not like this."

Gideon opened his mouth to ask, but then a flash of thoughts sped across his brain. A million ideas all chained together into a tangled mesh of nonsense. Those ideas, somehow now a physical concept as real as any other, sped away from him, granting him a literal perspective on the bigger picture they made.

Power like heat from a coal stove radiated from the shifting green mass. Even so far away, Gideon could not make out a single discernible shape, then a hole opened next to the green. In the same way that these green thoughts were solid, the hole was everything that matter was not. In the realest sense of the words, the hole was *Not Real*. It started to swallow the green as Gideon's viewpoint raced toward it.

There, at the fringe of the green, tendrils flowing into his body, hovered Vox. White haired and blank eyed, chains surrounded him like an ever-shifting mass of swords and shields. Across from Vox, on a platform made of the very substance of creation, stood Gideon and his companions. As they fought, pushing Vox ever closer to the hole in reality, more of the green flowed into him.

When Vox finally fell and the hole consumed the green, Gideon saw what he had missed before: Vox never touched the

41

hole. Instead, the green consumed him just shy of the edge of nothingness.

Gideon snapped back to reality and his eyes fixated on a falling leaf, a little island of calm amid the sounds of violence and death ringing in the darkness. His brain knew that leaf had only descended a few centimeters since his vision started.

He locked eyes with Catherine as a wisp of sapphire smoke drifted out of her eyes, lingering on the windless air. That it was her doing was obvious, so he asked the next question birthed by his vision.

"Vox has a piece of Corinthus?"

She nodded. "The last piece, unless he's released it, much like Umbras has a piece of myself."

"So he's drunk from Mímisbrunnr and I haven't?"

She nodded slowly as a smile crept across her face. "Wrong spring, but you're correct in spirit."

Gideon did his best to return the sly grin as the reality of his current situation slowly continued to creep in. "I wasn't aware Artemis had a well from which to drink." He paused. "Catherine."

She met his eyes for a moment, but did not reply to his comment beyond a slight twist of her lips that might have been a smile. Instead, Catherine gestured in the direction the soldier went. "Umbras is out there with those soldiers. He'll take care of them."

Gideon raised an eyebrow. "And me? I'm to help you fight this Taimethis character, yes? Why don't we take out Vox first? Surely you, Umbras, and myself would overpower him quickly."

"We would, but Taimethis would likely escape. Have you

42

ever read those stories, or seen the movies I suppose, where the hero ventures alone into the castle to take out the dragon or the demon or whatever the villain is while the armies battle outside?"

Gideon nodded. "I never much cared for that particular plot device."

Catherine laughed. "That's too bad, because you're in one of those stories right now."

Gideon spared another glance into the darkness, ears leading his eyes to the particular patch of black where Umbras and the saber-armed man were fighting Vox.

Turning back to Catherine, he shook his head and laughed. "Lead on, but tell me something."

She turned as the wind picked up, whipping her lace-trimmed half skirt out to the side like a cloak. Without checking to see if Gideon was following, she replied, "ask away."

"Why here?"

"Because this is where Vox is and where Vox is, Taimethis will be."

"Are you sure?"

Her shoulders tensed. "I can feel him, Gideon."

"I can accept that, but why *here*?"

"Trust me, I'm going to ask." Even with her back turned, the sound of her voice carried the tension of a taught neck and clenched teeth.

Gideon sped up. "Catherine, I," he placed his hand on her shoulder. Beneath the brown silk of her bolero, her skin was inhumanly hot to the touch, like that of someone fresh from the sauna. She had not been so warm before. Gideon reasoned it was a byproduct of whatever she was doing to prepare for the fight ahead.

If she was aware of the unnatural temperature of her skin, Catherine said nothing about it. Instead, she quirked that same perplexing smile. "Yes?"

"I assume you've got a plan."

Her expressive features fell for a moment. "I have," she admitted, "part of a plan."

"Part?" He tightened his grip on her shoulder, conscious of her sauna-hot body temperature and his complete inability to stop her from moving if she did not want him to.

She relented, however, and her temperature started to cool. "In this reality, Taimethis could eradicate you with little effort."

Gideon narrowed his eyes. "But he won't?"

"Oh, he would. Your last sight would be a ravening surge of energy, from either his eyes or his hands. It would," the smirk returned, "depend on his mood."

"Comforting."

"You fought Corinthus."

"Corinthus could not shoot death rays out of his eyes."

"He could have, but when you fought him, you did so in a place that put you on equal footing."

Gideon eyed her. "And you're going to take us there." It was not a question.

"It won't be easy," she admitted. "I can't just *take* him away."

A smile spread across Gideon's face. "We've got to trick him."

"That's where you come in. Standing this close to me, you're masked by my," she stopped, thinking.

"Aura?" Gideon offered.

"That's not quite right, but it'll do. You're more like a candle standing next to a star. No offense."

"I'll decide if I'm offended after we're sure I'm going to survive."

Catherine laughed, smiling. "I knew I went to find you for a reason."

"But," he said, "if we're to stop Taimethis, I'm sure there would have been others more suited to your task."

"I don't believe so," she replied. The enigma that was her facial expression deepened. A dozen emotions flickered by in an instant. Her black lips curled into something that might have been a smile if Gideon had been capable of understanding her mind just then.

Before he could say anything about it, she indicated the pistol in his hand and the pocket where he kept his portal controller. She then said, "you have two weapons. Three, if we count your mind. Allow me to give you another."

"Ano—"

His question was cut short as Catherine pulled him in close and her lips found his. Her skin, still far too warm to be human, seemed to leech heat into his body in those few glorious seconds.

He stumbled away as she released him. Shaking his head, the fog cleared, and Gideon asked, "for luck?"

"No," she replied. "Well, perhaps. But now you possess a very tiny amount of my power concentrated in a shield. It will do two things. First, it will hide you from Taimethis until he can see you directly."

"Useful."

"Second," she continued, "it will protect you *once* from his power." Her eyes widened. "Now run, hide. You'll know when the time is right."

Without hesitation, Gideon turned and sprinted into the darkness. A hair-raising feeling on his neck told him which way to go. As long as he kept that feeling of power at his back, his path took him away from Catherine and, he assumed, Taimethis.

After a minute's run through dark trees, Gideon slowed. His eyes were good, but breaking his nose on a tree trunk would be a bad start to this fight. He turned to his right, moving slowly now as the feeling of power pricked at the side of his neck.

Another minute passed and a brilliant blue glow, the same color as the smoke he had seen from Catherine's eyes after his vision, lit up part of the forest. A few meters away from the blue glow, a crimson light source appeared. Neither brightened from dim to full, rather it was like someone switched on two electric lights, instant and without warning.

"Catherine," a male voice said. He spoke with a warm, honeyed baritone as though addressing an old friend.

"Cut the crap, Taimethis," Catherine's voice replied.

Taimethis tisked. "Such rudeness. I came to an empty planet so I wouldn't have to worry about any collateral damage while teaching Vox to control his power, and what do I find? I'm not here more than an hour and you've got people trying to kill him."

"Vox is a murderer, Taimethis."

"Vox is a man driven insane by a gift our people gave him. I'm trying to fix that."

"Corinthus didn't give him a 'gift.' Corinthus used him like a puppet."

"*After* he went mad. Don't tell me you never picked up on it?" Taimethis chuckled.

"I never met Vox before Corinthus and now that we've touched him, none of us can go back to stop that moment."

"At any rate, Catherine, I just wanted to help him understand. Surely you can sympathize. Where would, what's his name now? Umbras? Where would Umbras be without your guidance?"

"There's a very human expression, Taimethis. Apples and Oranges."

"They're the same, Vox and Umbras. I don't care what you think about what Corinthus did, but I'm trying to undo that."

"By training him to use his power."

"He certainly can't be rid of it, so why shouldn't I?"

"I'm going to stop you."

"From what? Training a single man?"

The blue glow flared. "From turning him into a weapon!"

The red glow enlarged and brightened, threatening to overpower the blue for a moment. "Look me in the eyes and tell me that Umbras is different! Tell me that, Catherine! Tell me your human is different! You fed him your power just like Astenath did with Vox!"

The blue glow dimmed for a moment and Gideon's heart skipped. Adrenaline dumped into his veins and he readied himself to spring. One more breath and he would move. His hand tightened on the grip of his gun. One more breath.

Catherine's blue aura flared, eclipsing Taimethis's red for a moment. "Umbras asked! Vox did not!"

Taimethis roared and his voice echoed in Gideon's bones. "You're not going to stop me!"

The red flared again and an earsplitting whine shot through the air. The pitch dropped as Catherine's aura brightened as well, then a pillar of red light wrapped in a swirl of blue shot away from the clearing and lanced through the sky.

"I've seen less subtle signals before," Gideon muttered, starting to creep closer. He turned so that the twin auras were in front of him as he moved sideways through the trees.

Several more lances of red sped into the sky. He supposed Catherine was redirecting those beams of energy upwards and that, thanks to her gift, even she had no idea where he was at any given moment.

That's just what I need, Gideon thought to himself, for her to deflect one of those beams right into my face.

It took him five full minutes to get close enough to actually see what was going on. To one side, Catherine moved and flowed like a dancer in her steampunk clothing. Swirls of sapphire energy trailed her hands and feet as she moved. With her back to him, the next thing he noticed what that she lost the little hat that had been pinned to her hair—after the fight, she was going to be angry about that, he was sure.

Then, Catherine turned and Gideon's jaw fell open. Her face with its dramatic makeup was lit up by twin torrents of blue flame that poured from her eyes.

Across the little clearing Taimethis moved in straight lines and with sharp, hard movements. In his hands he held a staff with rings dangling from the head like a Shinto *shakujo*. He swung it in great arcs like a halberd, and it trailed sharp blades of red when it moved. Taimethis was dressed in what might have passed for

48

relaxed wear on the earth of his childhood. White jodhpurs terminated into black boots. Above that, Taimethis wore a black shirt topped with a red waistcoat that was a near match for the twin crimson stars that had replaced his eyes.

The two of them moved around each other, sending shocks through the air whenever they connected a blow. Catherine hit far more than she was hit, but her flowing style seemed incapable of delivering the sort of literally-earthshaking blows as Taimethis.

Gideon watched for another minute, trying to figure out exactly how he, a mortal who most definitely could not stand up to that kind of power, was going to intervene.

Taimethis fired off another beam from his hand. It struck Catherine directly, burning red against the blue swirling from her hands. The force of it pushed her back before she was able to redirect it into the sky again. When the mingling purple smoke cleared, part of Catherine's jacket and skirt had been burned away. Gideon felt a pang of guilt watching her move, knowing that dodging those attacks was likely an easy task if she did not have to keep him safe.

Which, again, made Gideon wonder *why*.

He had little time to ponder that thought as the bones of a strategy coalesced in his mind. Withdrawing the portal controller from his pocket, Gideon dropped quietly into a crouch and set his gun on the ground. A few tweaks to the settings and he was able to open a portal on the far side of the clearing. Back in the darkness where no one could see, it would wait for seventy seconds before dissipating in a thunderclap and ruining his chances for a surprise attack.

Another tweak to the device's settings and the next portal would open in front of him. He disabled the controller's safeties, allowing one-handed operation, and held it in his right hand. With his left, he picked up the revolver from the ground and took careful aim.

With his thumb, Gideon toggled the selector for the larger of the gun's two barrels. He exhaled and gently squeezed the trigger. The gun hummed for half a heartbeat as impossible forces poured themselves into the focusing array and a dark purple lance skewered Taimethis in the shoulder.

The gravity beam blew away Taimethis's shoulder joint and a good portion of his chest and neck. The wound poured crimson steam onto the ground. In an instant, Taimethis's eyes locked on Gideon's location and their glow brightened a thousandfold.

His fingers moved too slowly toward the control and impossible heat and agony washed over him. In that moment, Gideon gained a new appreciation for the term "pain" as Taimethis's wrathful counterattack seemed to burn him to his very soul.

That moment passed and he felt a sudden lightness in his chest. He burned on the inside, pain welling up in his mouth until he spat out blue fire. Alive and energized thanks to Catherine's power, Gideon pulled the trigger again. This second shot took Taimethis in the thigh, destroying it like the first had his shoulder.

Rather than fall, he stood on one leg and a pillar of red smoke. From his destroyed shoulder, a tendril lashed out at Catherine so quickly that even she had trouble deflecting the attack.

Taimethis's eyes flared again, and this time Gideon's fingers moved a little faster. The portal opened a scant few centimeters in front of his face. Linked to the other, Taimethis's eye beams poured into the hole in space only to reappear behind his back.

Taimethis's own power ripped through his body, obliterating what remained and then scorching a path through the trees.

When Catherine turned, Gideon saw part of her face had been burned away by Taimethis's earlier attacks. Instead of the blood and gore he expected, what smiled back at him was half the beautiful human face he expected and half a visage of brilliant blue, like crystal lit from within.

They locked eyes, or Gideon locked his eyes on Catherine's human eye and a bright portion where her other eye should be, and he nodded. She swirled her hands around, dancing a network of lines into existence.

On the other side of the clearing, the red smoke that was Taimethis was already reforming into a human shape. Another moment passed while red raced with blue and Gideon leveled his revolver at the red cloud. He fired again and what might have been an arm vanished from the core of the red. The other growth slowed as a new arm took its place in moments.

"Gideon!" Catherine called in a voice of wind and rain. One hand held something that looked to Gideon's eyes like a horse's reins, only made of blue fire. The other beckoned him closer and he broke into a sprint, careful to keep his gun trained on Taimethis.

He reached out to her beckoning hand, took it. Her other hand pulled on the cord of fire and the world vanished.

***

Gideon fell forever. Beside him, Catherine's human form knitted itself back together, blue crystal concealed beneath human flesh once again. Something else lingered there, visible behind reality. Gideon did not know for how long he tried to focus on it, whatever "it" was, but eventually he started to see past

Catherine's human form and to the luminous being beyond it.

She was beautiful and terrible all at the same time, like the light of a star wrapped in a cup of tea and carried in the hand of the apocalypse.

Before he could ask how long the drop would last, he stood on solid ground again. He did not impact it, nor was there any transition between falling and not-falling. One instant, Gideon and Catherine plunged through infinity, and the next he stood on a platform of stone that stretched as far as his eye could see.

"Where are we?"

Catherine, fully human-seeming again aside from the unnerving blue flames pouring from her eyes, regarded him silently. Distracted by her fiery eyes, Gideon did not notice for a moment that she finally shed the decorative, but ultimately poorly designed for combat, clothing she wore before. Now, Catherine dressed in a bodysuit of deep black, featureless save for a brilliant sapphire at her throat.

Gideon began to sense a theme and unconsciously touched the sapphire blue cravat that encircled his own neck. Coincidences, he reminded himself, did not happen.

When Catherine spoke, her voice still carried undercurrents that sounded like a distant thunderstorm. "We're between realities where only thought and power exist."

Gideon raised an eyebrow. "Impossible. Even the Inn *exists*."

"Have you ever played early twenty-first century video games, Gideon?"

Surprised by the apparent non-sequitur, Gideon cocked his head to one side. "Some, why?"

"A lot of them had glitches that would turn reality inside out.

Colors would be reversed, or the controls wouldn't work right. Sometimes the world would shift, appear and disappear, at random. You know what I'm talking about, right?"

Gideon slowly nodded. "Negative levels, yes."

Catherine indicated the blank landscape with a wave of her hand. "This is the realm of thought, where reality is only limited by what you can imagine."

"And Taimethis?"

"He's here somewhere."

Gideon shook his head. "No, I mean what does this place do for him?"

"It's more about what it can do for you, Gideon. Here, you're no less powerful than I am."

With a little more emphasis, Gideon repeated himself. "And Taimethis?"

Catherine closed her eyes for a moment. The effect was strange as what appeared to be human eyelids, made of nothing more than flesh and blood, perfectly concealed the streams of blue fire for a few seconds. When she opened them, Catherine said, "Taimethis can imagine quite a lot."

As though summoned, Taimethis now stood a few meters off to Gideon's left. He had regenerated his clothes and staff. He stood with his staff resting between arms folded across his chest. Like Catherine, the only thing to mark him as inhuman in that moment were his eyes. They glowed a deep crimson red, twin smokeless hearts of fire.

"Why?" he asked in his voice of honey.

Catherine wheeled on him, hands coming up in guard. Blue symbols, illegible to Gideon's eyes, swarmed around them in

53

rings. He drew and leveled his revolver, aiming at Taimethis's face.

Calmly, Taimethis unfolded his arms and set the butt of his staff on the stone ground. "I'm going to ask you again, Catherine, and I at least would like an answer before you try to uncarnate me. Need I remind you that *you* came after *me*. I didn't seek out this confrontation, nor did I throw the first blow. You've dogged me for a dozen cycles now and I *demand* to know *why.*"

With the sound of a storm, Catherine replied, "you're dangerous, Taimethis."

"I?" he demanded, then repeated himself. "*I?* Corinthus is dangerous. Astenath is dangerous! I'm trying to fix the damage they've caused, or I would be except you continue to follow me. You are a blight!"

The sound of rain became the crash of a tsunami. "You've destroyed universes!"

Gideon's blood ran cold. He might be immortal, but experience taught him over and over that he was most definitely not invincible. He supposed he was somewhat more durable than the average man, but even that was nothing compared to the kinds of power facing him now.

Yet options remained. Gideon forced himself to remember the fact that he had a weapon powerful enough to damage Taimethis's human form—human shell? Gideon asked himself. Just what were these people?—even in the real universe. Catherine's cryptic instructions rang in his ears and Gideon relaxed through nothing less than force of will.

He focused on something simple: a fissure. For a moment, nothing happened. Gideon grit his teeth and imagined it again, envisioning even the smallest detail. He saw the pattern in the ground as it opened, heard the roaring of rock tearing itself apart, felt the rush of air as the land heaved upward and snapped shut on Taimethis's body.

Then, exactly as he saw it in his mind, it happened. Distracted by his argument with Catherine, Taimethis did not react fast enough to the sudden attack and any retort he had planned was drowned by the thundercrack of stone slamming back together.

"He's not done yet," Catherine warned.

"I wouldn't expect him to be." With a smile, Gideon said, "what fun would this be if he went down that easily?"

"Just be alert, Gideon."

Watching the landscape whose gray stone now gradually tuned a sandy red, he asked, "how many times have you fought him, exactly?"

"Like this?"

"Yes."

"This is the first."

"He said you'd been following him?"

"In the real universe, where he can't kill me."

"And now?"

"Just like you're as powerful as we are, we're as mortal as you."

Gideon grimaced. "That's reassuring. I wasn't expecting to have to kill a god before dinner. Is he really as dangerous as you say?"

Catherine nodded. "I wasn't lying. Taimethis destabilized time by meddling too much. In an instant, a trillion trillion lives," she snapped her fingers, and Gideon flinched, "gone."

A knot formed in Gideon's stomach. "How?"

"He changed too many things, reset events too many times trying to get the outcome he wanted."

"How is that different from what I, or any of us living in the Inn, do?"

"You move time around. There's still a universe where the crew of the *Staraveth* arrive at a dead, frozen world. In that universe, their planet plays an important role in a thousand events through history.

"So why me?"

"Why you specifically, or why *not* someone like Umbras?"

"Both."

"For the former, it's because Umbras recommended you. I meant it when I said that earlier. As for the latter, let's say that Umbras and I respect one another but we are perhaps the multiverse's worst partners for something like this."

"Remind me to..." Gideon trailed off as the ground beneath his feet rumbled and spoke.

"Your human learns quick, Dart-Thrower."

Through gritted teeth, the storm that was Catherine replied, "do *not* call me that." To Gideon, she added, "be ready."

"For?"

She pointed. "That."

Gideon pivoted to face the direction she indicated, gun at the ready. He instinctively fired off a shot from the gravity lens at what he thought was a nearby, man-sized target. The beam sped across space for some distance before the figure uncurled an impossibly long arm and swatted it away.

"Remember my video game metaphor?"

Gideon nodded, resisting the automatic urge to fire another shot.

"Let's just say, Taimethis hacks."

"Can we beat him?"

"He's been beaten before."

"By you?"

"I was there."

"Comforting."

Within the space of a heartbeat, reality changed. Up became sideways as a massive wall of stone appeared in front of Gideon's face, moving toward him at impossible speeds. The stone struck him, sending Gideon flying through the air like a discarded baseball. Somewhere beneath the sound of the avalanche, he heard Catherine yelling his name.

Sailing through the air, Gideon again reminded himself of Catherine's instructions. He pictured flight, controlling his movement in the air with nothing more than the desire to move in any direction.

Abruptly, he came to a midair stop, hovering what seemed to be a dozen meters above the ground.

What he assumed to be Taimethis loomed in the distance, impossibly far and yet still uncomfortably close. A torso that might have been human-shaped sat in the middle of too many limbs. Four arms swept the sky in every direction and instead of legs, he now possessed serpentine coils that merged with the red stone. Instead of a head, the red glow of Taimethis's eyes floated in empty space above his shoulders.

57

Gideon realized he dropped his gun when Taimethis's snake coil sent him flying. Instead of looking for it, he simply imagined it being back in his hand, and it was.

One of Taimethis's impossibly long arms swept toward him, parting the air with a sonic boom. Gideon concentrated on the idea of flight, of dodging, and veered out of the hand's path. In the same moment, he squeezed his gun's trigger, piercing the index finger of Taimethis's hand.

Recoil, normally manageable on the ground, pushed Gideon backward and broke his momentary concentration. His mind immediately remembered that humans did not fly and he plummeted to the stony ground next to Catherine.

She gestured and a blue glow formed under Gideon's feet, lifting and pushing him away as the ground where he fell formed into another snake coil. Another appeared under her feet and she rose into the air after him.

Standing on Catherine's platform, Gideon imagined great pillars of stone rising from the ground like spring-loaded bolts. They would snap out, strike Taimethis, possibly even pierce him, over and over again until the stone monstrosity crumbled.

Nothing happened.

Gideon tried again, thinking about the sound each one of the pillars would make. The grinding noise of stone on stone filled his mind, then the avalanche sound as they broke him apart. Clear and vivid this time, sixteen pillars leapt from the ground at once, all speeding for Taimethis's chest. If he was half as big as he seemed, Gideon's attack moved as fast as a bullet.

Then they stopped, quivered, and each of the sixteen pillars snapped at the base. They hovered there before swirling around Taimethis and coming to settle behind his back like a set of skeletal wings.

Now, Gideon understood what Catherine meant. Taimethis had become the ground itself. Any attempt to use the vast plain of stone would fail. Simply standing on it would be death.

So, he pulled lances out of the air itself, focusing it into sharp bursts and striking at Taimethis's stony arms like a hundred hammers. The stone that made up his body creaked and shuddered as dust motes the size of mountains fell away.

To his left, Catherine drew a long arc in the air that solidified into a bow of sapphire light. Arrows appeared in her hand, ready to draw and be loosed. She took aim at the nearest of Taimethis's four arms, loosing an arrow that sped through the air like a shaft of moonlight.

Gideon aimed his lances of air at the spot Catherine hit, focusing them more and more on a steadily smaller area until the palm cracked and a world of debris fell a thousand kilometers to the ground.

Catherine drew her bow again, fighting to stay stable as Taimethis's tails snapped at her like whips. Automatically, Gideon aimed and fired his LeMat at the spot where the stone serpents broke from the ground. They writhed and pulled away from Catherine's platform as the focused gravity beam pierced them both.

One of Taimethis's hands swept by them, breaking Gideon's air lances like glass and causing enough turbulence to knock him from his platform. Reflexively, he fired at the hand as it trailed away from them. It shuddered, but continued its course through the heavens.

Gideon remembered that he could fly here at the same instant that he impacted solid stone. For a moment, he thought he fell

59

back to the ground, but then realized that the gentle curves of the city-sized plateau of stone were in fact the contours of Taimethis's hand.

He came to that realization moments before fingers the size of starships curled up and over him. Gideon shot a hole in one with his gun and dust rained down on him, but Taimethis's monstrous grip continued to close.

The image of a sycamore pod filled his mind, propelled on a curl of blue crystal. Gideon closed his eyes and vividly called to memory the sensation of trying to crush one of the spiny seed pods in his hand. To that, Gideon added the idea of millions of nails and reality coalesced around his body to form a protective spiked metal shell.

His next thought was of chains and ropes. Gideon envisioned binding Taimethis's stone hand, of pulling the fist tighter against himself until he heard the creaking and groaning of stone. He felt the pressure on his protective shell as though it were him. It increased, bending the spines, and he continued to focus on the idea of chains binding the great hand.

Pressure continued to mount until it became pain. Gideon, embodying the spiked shell, felt the force in his bones. It drove him to his knees inside the shell and he knew that if Taimethis's hand remained intact much longer, it would crush him.

Then, as suddenly as his protection appeared, the pressure disappeared. Gideon dismissed the shield in time to see Catherine standing on her platform, already pivoting away to take aim at the next stone hand. The cool glow of one of her arrows lingered on the broken bits of Taimethis's fingers.

His entire hand crumbled and Gideon was again falling. This time, he remembered flight early and brought himself back into the air and set down on Taimethis's wrist. More distance separated him from Taimethis's body than separated the Sun from Earth and another of Taimethis's impossibly long arms bore down on him. The hand glowed a deep red, burning with atmospheric heating as the moon-sized palm drew closer.

Taimethis's hand stopped a thousand kilometers above him. The glow in the palm brightened as solar fire leapt across interstellar distances. Hydrogen plasma hot enough to reduce him to ash superheated the air around him and his clothes burst into flames.

Pain bit into Gideon's skin, but he fixated on a single thought. Aloud, he said, "I am fireproof."

The flames on his clothes went out for a moment, then reignited as the solar flare drew closer and the air got hotter.

Finally, Gideon understood. Taimethis constantly grew larger, using his arms and tails to distract his opponents until he was so large that they could never reach him. Even now, the hand he and Catherine shattered was reforming itself out of superheated metals cast off by the solar flare bearing down on him.

"It's all a damned *feint*," Gideon growled.

He imagined the distance shrinking. The millions of kilometers between his perch on Taimethis's wrist and the colossus's torso shrank. The distances grew again as Taimethis realized what Gideon was doing and fought him.

The solar flare stretched and shrank, first a match, then the end of the universe, and back again a thousand times. It slowed as space itself warped. Catherine's platform, visible now only as a glowing blue speck against the red flare, circled it, deflecting the monstrous fireball.

Taimethis pushed against Gideon, stretching space again, and this time Gideon allowed it to happen. Taimethis grew, his arm stretching a billion kilometers from end to end and a thousand kilometers thick. Gideon allowed that to happen as well, envisioning now that he simply stood on Taimethis's torso, looking up at his eyes.

Trusting Catherine to occupy Taimethis's arms, Gideon opened his own eyes and found himself face to face with the man again. Rather than speak to him, even to threaten him, Taimethis leapt into action. His eyes flared, twin beams of destruction, but Gideon was prepared this time.

Gideon threw his right leg to his left side, pulling himself out of the way of Taimethis's attack. The red god's aim was off, distracted as he was fighting Catherine with his stone colossus body, and Gideon took aim with his LeMat.

The gravity beam obliterated Taimethis's human torso. The beams ceased as his head, arms, and legs dissipated into red smoke. Under his feet, the stone god's torso cracked and started to fall apart.

Catherine appeared at his side, wordlessly weaving blue crystal around the red mist that was all that remained of Taimethis. She danced the cage into being with a frenzy Gideon did not expect, but was too slow. The red smoke escaped, but instead of reforming either man or monster, it simply vanished into the air.

Gideon sank to the ground beneath him. Intellectually he knew the stone was falling, but the ground was a million, million kilometers down. He could take a second to breathe first. "Is he dead?"

Catherine shook her head angrily. "No." A smile spread across her face. "But he's wounded."

Gideon laughed. "Does that mean we won?"

Catherine sat down next to him, her eyes still billowing blue fire. She smiled and with the voice of a storm said, "yes."

"Good." Gideon stood, offering a hand to Catherine to help her to her feet "Let's go home, then. We missed dinner."

CHAOS CANDY

-by-
Amie Gibbons

For my kitteh

Because he doesn't run when he sees the darkness

He stays and has my back while I face it.

CHAPTER ONE

Lindsey Pratt had always been a bitch. Now she was just a bitch with a badge.

Zee crossed her arms, slouching in her chair and sizing the bitch up over her desk.

They'd met on their first day of Parata University. Zee had barely joined with her order a month before classes started, and Lindsey's had been together for about six months and had had a chance to learn the basics of magic.

And Lindsey thought that made them *so* superior.

Witches joined into orders of five elements after they turned eighteen: fire, water, air, earth, and multi. Their powers couldn't come on until they were eighteen due to the spell the Parata government put over the world, and even then, they didn't come on until five witches were drawn together and formed a bonded order. Zee's didn't form until she was nearly twenty-one, making her one of the older beginners.

Lindsey had showed Zee up in Potions, Zee broke her pointy little nose in martial arts, and after that, it was *on*.

Lindsey won their ongoing bitchfest when she dated Zee's order's water Brad, and then broke his heart.

Three years after his death, Zee still *hated* her for that.

Fire witches held grudges like that.

And now Lindsey wanted her help?

Oh, this was rich.

Zee's office was a converted living room. The thick white carpet set off the squishy gold and black chairs. Little froufrou, but she didn't decorate it. Then again, she wasn't about to change it either.

You didn't change things your dead best friend decorated.

"Let me see if I've got this straight," Zee said. "You want to hire me? And it's not through the Agency?"

Lindsey flushed and worked her jaw for a second before she forced it into an obviously painful smile. "Yes."

If she was swallowing eight years of rivalry, it had to be good. It couldn't hurt to find out what was going on.

"What's the job?" Zee asked.

"My order's fire's missing. I need you to find him."

That was it?

Zee knew Jarred. He was a playboy. He was probably in the Trenster reality, hanging on the beach and downing mojitos while he hit on everything in a bikini.

"Was he arrested and ran?" Zee asked.

Lindsey's left eye twitched and she shook her head, making her blond curls dance around her chin.

Zee smiled. "Then why are you coming to me?"

She scowled, meeting Zee's eyes with fire. "Fuck, you're going to make this difficult, aren't you?"

"Why don't you start with explaining why you don't just use the Agency's resources to find him yourself? You're an agent. Missing persons are part of your job. I'm a bounty hunter. They're only my job if they're running from you guys."

Lindsey leaned forward, resting clenched hands on Zee's desk. "Exactly."

Zee blinked, pursing her lips. Jarred was actually on the run? She couldn't imagine Jarred being in trouble with the Agency for anything serious.

Maybe with the human police in the main reality for speeding tickets… or picking up a prostitute. But something Parata authorities would care about?

"Really?" Zee asked.

"There's a warrant out for his arrest. The Agency has people looking for him. I need to find him first and prove he's innocent."

Hairy black holes, this was getting good. "What's the charge?"

"Inter-reality smuggling."

Big whoop. With the Agency's regulations, who *didn't* smuggle?

"Drug trafficking…"

That made Zee's eyebrows shoot up. Drug smuggling?

Lindsey licked her lips, taking off a layer of shimmery gloss. "And conspiracy to commit murder."

"And now we get to it. So that would be charg*es*?"

Lindsey's hands went limp like they'd been shot. "Please don't be a bitch, Zee. This is hard enough. You want me to beg, I will. You want three, five times your going rate, it's yours." Her voice cracked and her big baby blues sparkled.

Damn. Tears. Zee didn't do tears.

"Consider me de-bitched. Just tell me what happened."

"That's the thing. I don't know. Last night, Secretary Jolnavich came to my place, asking where Jarred was. He said there's evidence Jarred's involved with the Chaos Kings, and when he went to bring him in for questioning, Jarred wasn't there."

"Wait." Zee held up a finger. "Chaos Kings? As in the only gang of witches powerful and smart enough to evade the Agency and smuggle Chaos Candy into the main reality?"

Lindsey nodded.

"As in the punk asses who spread that drug around humans, witches, and vampires alike. As in the bastards who've paid off and memory wiped more agents than they've killed, which is saying something. As in the gang so bad they make the Crips and Bloods look like fucking rabbis. Those Chaos Kings?"

"I know it looks bad."

"No. Mullets look bad. This looks *messy*. The Agency is desperate to stop the Kings. Any lead turns them into the Gestapo and KGB rolled into one… more so than they already are. What do they have on Jarred?"

"They wouldn't tell me. My order and I aren't allowed within a mile of this case. I've talked to everyone I know. If any of them are on the case or know anything, they aren't talking. Agents could've found Chaos Candy at his place, money somehow traced back to some other lead they have, or just saw him talking to a suspected member of the Kings. I haven't heard from Jarred since Friday in the main reality, and there was nothing out of the ordinary then."

It was Saturday. Parata ran parallel to the main reality. Witches lived out their lives in the human world, then went into the pocket reality of Parata to repeat the week and work on magical studies and exploring alternate realities.

"So Jarred's been missing for a day and didn't make it into Parata for the week? He could've been sleeping off a bender and missed the opening for the week."

"Does that mean you won't help me?"

Zee held up a finger. "I never said that. How do you know Jarred's innocent?"

"Because I know *him*. He might do recreational human drugs here and there, but he'd *never* help get that kind of poison into the world, especially not when humans could get it. Zee, you know he's a playboy, sure, but he's not a bad person. Chaos Candy kills its users. It shouldn't even be considered a drug. It's poison that makes you high first, that's all."

How did Zee know she was going to say something like that?

A warm weight settled against Zee's leg and she scratched the big head without looking down. Sasha whined and licked her hand, tail thumping against the side of the desk.

Lindsey wrinkled her nose at the giant Husky and Zee smirked.

"Cracking into the Kings would be a serious coup. The Agency would be falling over themselves to thank me."

If Zee got any info regarding the Kings, the Agency might even let her run the bounty hunter course she'd proposed last year. The arrogant, controlling bastards said it wasn't necessary. Anyone wanting to learn those skills could learn them from the Agency and become an agent. They had no qualms about hiring her when they needed help tracking down a criminal though.

Funny, that.

"So you'll do it?" Lindsey sounded way too hopeful.

"Yes."

Her smile was brilliant, absolute gratitude. Oh God, she was grateful to her nemesis since she'd agreed to help her friend.

I might have to like her after this.

Zee was a sucker for loyalty.

"Why me?" Zee asked.

"What?"

"For this job. You could've gone to the fugitive apprehension branch of the Agency. I know more than a few people in there who would be glad to find Jarred and keep it under wraps if the price was right. Why me?"

"You're going to make me say it?"

"Yes."

"*Fine*. First, because you're one of the best. Second, because those people who'd take a bribe from me are the same ones who'd take one from the Kings. You wouldn't. You've never taken a bribe and everyone from agents to vampires knows you have integrity and you'd never turn your back on that."

Zee nodded. Couldn't argue any of those.

"But the main reason I came to you is because you quit the Agency. *Nobody* quits. The Agency has the power, the resources, and the best working for them. You get perks and leeway in the Agency other witches don't, and you left it all and started a bounty hunter firm to *compete* with the Agency. No one has done that in the four hundred years of Parata's existence."

Zee nodded.

She'd left the Agency exactly because that's how they worked. Parata's government had become so totalitarian they made the old USSR look reasonable. Those in the Agency, i.e., the party, got special privileges, different rules applied to them, and there was no competition, meaning the government had gotten fat and happy the last hundred years or so, and the people were so used to it, they just worked around the rules.

And Zee wanted to burn the whole establishment down and start the government over with the ideals of freedom and individualism Parata had been built on.

But most people thought that was kind of extreme.

"You have connections the Agency can't even hope for because you turned your back on them," Lindsey said, "and the magical underground loves that. And I need those balls and connections right now."

Zee nodded.

"I'm in," she said. "Here's the terms. Anything you know about Jarred, I need to. I'll need full access to his homes and offices, here and in the main reality. Do not tell anyone you hired me, not even the rest of your order. Pay me half up front. Then stay out of my way."

"Have you done this before? Investigated a crime?"

Zee kept her face blank. If the Agency knew...

"I'm a bounty hunter. That requires a certain amount of investigation. Can you live with my terms?"

"Yes." Lindsey stood and held out her hand.

Zee stood and shook it.

And just like that, she was on the case.

CHAPTER TWO

The sun was just rising over the projected mountains in Parata as Zee left her office.

Both the mountains and the sun were projected into Parata. It was a witch-built pocket reality maybe the size of an eastern state and Zee's office was near the edge next to the campus, meaning it would've been quite a walk to Agency Headquarters if she had to walk.

Zee teleported to the Agency's steps after changing into a more badass outfit than her usual work attire of slacks and silky tops.

When in doubt, she'd go with badass.

She'd put on her favorite red leather pants, black tank and army boots.

The tank left the scars on her right shoulder and arm bare for all to see. Scars were practically non-existent in Parata, where the doctors could fix almost anything except death and taxes.

Made everyone look twice and wonder what the hell could create scars doctors couldn't heal but still couldn't kill her.

The Agency ran Parata. It was the police force, the legislature, the executive, and the judicial. No separation of powers.

No need for it, according to them.

Agency Headquarters was a love child between the Pantheon and modern innovation, a thirty-story circular glass ass coming out of a Greek temple front big enough to eat the actual Pantheon as an afternoon snack.

Zee walked up the wide steps and through the shield running

72

between the columns. It prevented teleporting and detected stored spells, potions, and anything metallic.

Which was why Zee's assorted knives, lock pics and batons were ceramic and hard plastic.

And very well concealed.

The lobby was rose colored marble, with masterpieces from dozens of different realities lining the two big walls, prime minister portraits on one side, and the most wanted posters on the other.

Zee walked straight to the back towards the circular desk guarding the opening to the hall holding the elevators. Agents walked through the shield guarding the hall. Visitors had to go through the receptionist or risk electrocution.

The weekend morning receptionist was Mary Anders.

And she loved Zee's stories.

Mary's head was bent over a textbook and she didn't look as Zee walked up.

"Hey," Zee said, knocking on the desktop.

"Oh, hey," she said, managing a smile even though there were bags under her eyes big enough to pack for a two-week trip to Europe in.

Ah, made Zee miss her schooldays.

Not.

She nodded down at the lines of equations running amuck over the pages. "What the hell is that?"

"Linear Algebra. See, you..."

"Please." Zee held up the mugs in defense. "Don't try to explain that shit to me again. I majored in history, remember?

73

Numbers are not my thing. Buzz me in?"

"Oh!" Her eyes focused on Zee's face and she frowned. "I got written up the last time I let you in."

"What'd they make you do?"

"One of the psych professors turned me into a rat and had me run through her new rat maze for three hours. I was coughing up hairballs for a day. Do real rats even get hairballs?"

Zee covered her mouth quickly. Poor Mary was claustrophobic. It wouldn't be nice to laugh.

"Did you hear about the big magic smack down in Rome last week?" Zee asked, leaning on the desk.

Mary's eyes inched up. If there was one thing Mary loved, it was gossip. "You know what happened?"

Zee nodded.

"You can't. The Agency's keeping it all hushed up. I haven't even heard anything about it here."

"I know one of the vampires that was involved. He told me everything. Everything the Agency doesn't want the rest of Parata to know."

Mary's eyes flew wide and Zee knew she had her.

Parata ran on magic and gossip. Witches loved gossip about vampires since they were the fringe dwellers of magic society. The Agency liked to spin them as the bad guys and that just made them more interesting to those not drinking the Kool-Aid.

# # #

A half an hour and one whispered story later, Zee stepped off the elevator on the nineteenth floor.

Agents' offices lined the hallway. With its intricate gold

74

wallpaper and soft carpeting, it looked more like a hotel's hall than a government's. Secretary Jolnavich was over the fugitive apprehension section. His office was at the end of the hall.

"Hey." Zee knocked on his open door and his head jerked up, blue eyes stabbing through her as he looked at her over his glasses like a disappointed grandpa.

"Who let you in?" he asked, gesturing for her to take a seat in front of his desk.

Zee stayed standing and crossed her arms.

"Jarred Krentz."

"No, he's on the run. I'm pretty sure he didn't let you in."

Zee grinned. "Cute. I want on the case."

"How did you hear about this?"

"I have my sources."

"We've got it covered."

"So you found him?"

"We will."

"That means no. You guys are swamped and you know it. Hire me and you can reassign the order looking for him. If I don't find him within two Parata weeks, I'll give you your money back."

And she did mean money. In Parata, the main currency was power. Want a latte from the coffee kiosk? Press your finger on the side of the espresso contraption and it's spelled to suck in a thread of magic to pay for the drink. Witches passing into Parata every Sunday lost a tiny bit of power to the government's treasury, which was used to maintain the reality and pay the public servants.

Death wasn't always certain when you lived in a magical reality, but taxes sure as shit were.

Zee had power naturally, plus tons more stored. She didn't need more of it nearly as much as she needed money that could be used in the main reality.

Jolnavich leaned forward, pressing his meaty palms to the desk. "You have never come to us looking to get on a case. Why this one?"

She let an evil grin tug up the corner of her mouth. "He's the Coyote Order's fire."

"We know that. So?"

"The Coyote's earth is an old school... *friend*."

He chuckled. "Let me guess, he showed you up in a class and you decided to hate him for eternity?"

"She, but other than that, yup."

He shook his head. "This isn't one guy running because he got caught smuggling. Krentz's in the Chaos Kings." He frowned. "You already knew that?"

That was the problem with trying to play Jolnavich. He was an empath and could feel her lack of surprise.

"I heard that's why he's being chased. What evidence do you have?"

"Nice try."

"If you put me on finding him, you can put the agents to better use following up the Kings' angle. I don't want to get caught up in that mess. I just want to haul Krentz's ass in."

"And this is just about an old grudge?"

She shrugged. "I haven't had a case in two weeks. I'm

bored."

He eyeballed her and she steeled her nerves, meeting his eyes.

Empaths couldn't read what wasn't there.

And nobody could bury emotions like an ex street kid who'd lost the four people who had been bound to her by magic closer than family.

He finally shook his head again. "You're hired."

"Thank-you. Case file, please."

"What do I look like? Your damn assistant? Copy it yourself. It's in the Zeus Order's office."

The coffee in her belly rolled up and she pressed her lips together. "The Zeuses are on this case?"

His smile was small and blew her evil one out of the water. "Did I forget to mention that? They're on point. The other order on this will be reassigned, but I have to keep at least one working. Eggs in one basket and all that."

"Were they on this case before or after I invaded your office?"

"Does it matter? They're on it now."

"You're a real bastard, Jolnavich."

"I know."

She left and grabbed the file out of the Zeus' office. Maybe, just maybe, whoever was originally on the case would keep working on it, and Jolnavich wouldn't go out of his way to tell the Zeus's he'd planned on reassigning them.

Wishful thinking, but she could only deal with one old enemy at a time.

CHAPTER THREE

"Chaos Candy is concocted with ingredients from many realities. None of which should have met," James said over the phone once Zee was back in the main reality for the week.

"Yeah, got that," Zee said, stroking Sasha's head with one hand and grabbing her wine with the other. "What I want to know is how, doc?"

He drew a sharp breath and Zee grinned.

"I have asked you repeatedly *not* to call me that, Sarah," he said, British accent clipping off the words making him sound even more of a prig than he already did.

"And I've asked you repeatedly not to call me Sarah." She chuckled. "So, what does Chaos Candy do that makes it so bad? What makes it different than normal drugs?"

"It disrupts the chemicals in the brain, bringing those who are unfortunate enough to try it to the edge of madness. This is no mere hallucinogen or euphoric. This drug enhances magic in our systems and gifts human users with magic. There is some mystery as to how, since the drug leaves little trace and taking one under its influence alive is... not feasible. However, we have found when ingested, it enhances not merely the magical potential in the person, but the magic potential in the reality."

"Oh boy. It makes more magic in the reality?"

"Yes. And while more energy is not usually a bad thing, here, the energy is tainted with chaos. When the energy is released, chaos ensues. Hence the name. There is no known way to control it, nor to capture those under its influence until it is out of their system, at which point they want more. They either obtain it, or they die of withdrawal."

"And I thought smoking was hard to kick. Any leads on the Chaos Kings?"

"None."

She rolled her eyes, scratching Sasha behind the ears. "James, if there's one person in this reality who would be able to find and track them, it's you. You're telling me you have nothing?"

"That is precisely what I am saying. I will see what information I can obtain; however, these people may as well be ghosts. They are not involved with the Smugglers' Society. No vampires in my network are working with them. Their modus operandi is to kidnap, bribe and blackmail witches into helping them smuggle, and then erasing their memories once they are finished with them. Those that resist are killed."

"You think that's what happened to Jarred?"

He sighed. "Why does the Agency believe he is involved with them?"

"One ingredient in Chaos Candy is a plant called the Urganta flower and the only known reality where it grows is Gort. A witch was arrested there last week. The Agency fed him a truth serum and he said he ran errands for the Kings on a case by case basis. One of his assignments was paying off agents. One of which was Jarred."

"Knowing their penchant for leaving their associates without their memories, I am not sure I would believe this man."

"Maybe they hadn't wiped him yet because he was still working for them?"

"Or perhaps they implanted false memories. Red herrings, if you will."

"See what you can find for me?"

"For you, of course."

"And how would you like your payment," she said, lowering her voice. "I'm thinking a-"

"I am quite certain I do not want to know what crassness would follow that thought. My usual fee will suffice."

She snorted. "You give vampires everywhere a bad name. Aren't you all supposed to be sexual deviants? You know I could teach you-"

"Sarah!"

"Awwwwww, sorry, I forgot sexual teasing offends your tender sensibilities."

"You are as crude and childish as Nathan."

"Yeah, I *miss* him. Tell him I say hi."

"Of course. I will call you with any information."

"Same here. Oh wait, can you try talking to your contact in the Agency? Something's fishy with the report and I want to know what they're saying amongst themselves."

"I would, however, that contact has ceased communications with me, and the last time I spoke with him, he told me to consume a bag of something quite graphic."

"Why do people say eat a bag of dicks like that's an insult?" Zee asked. "As long as the dicks are washed, a whole bag of them sounds like one hell of a party to me."

"Sarah! Must you be so crass?"

"What? I wouldn't bring up eating dicks if I wasn't willing to eat yours. I wouldn't tease you like that, and it's only polite."

"I... I..."

She could almost see his mouth working on the other side of the phone.

"I can not speak to you when you are like this," he finally sputtered.

Zee burst out laughing. "You are so much fun to tease. I've got to investigate some around here, but keep in touch? Tell me if you find anything?"

"Of course."

She hung up the phone, taking a long sip of wine and staring at the file spread over the coffee table.

"What now, baby?"

Sasha licked Zee's hand, setting her big head in her lap and pawing her leg.

"Yeah, yeah." Zee scratched her under her collar, grinning as Sasha's tail went nuts. "I know. There's always another angle. Just got to find it."

Zee wouldn't have made it through her order's death without Sasha.

If witches had familiars in their reality, she would've been Zee's.

# # #

Zee teleported to work near seven Monday morning.

In the main reality, she ran an occult bookstore in Green Valley, a nice community on the outer edge of Vegas. The store gave her the opportunity to cover her other, less legal activities. It took nearly a decade to build her rep, but every witch in the reality knew Zee's was the place to pick up the good stuff from the black market.

Zee unlocked, made coffee, and went through her messages. Most were on books she was trying to track down, but a few were coded ones about items witches were wondering if she had.

She was on her third cup and twelfth phone call when her assistant manager Penny Laundue bounced in. Zee set her up doing inventory and headed out, saying she was on the trail of a first edition Alice In Wonderland and Penny was in charge for the day.

# # #

The Coyote Order was based in Albuquerque. Zee teleported straight into Jarred's apartment since he lived alone.

She'd already been there before to ask him about a fugitive she was chasing since he was her favorite Coyote. His decorating style was very frat boy gone corporate. She guessed he kept the carpets and beanbags when he moved in after college and his order decorated the rest for him, but she'd never asked.

Now it looked like a scene from CSI: Parata.

The couches, chairs, and beanbags were all sliced open, their guts tossed around the room like the Hannibal Lector of furniture went after them. The shelves, lamps, plants, and knickknacks were overturned or thrown in corners. The walls were cut open every few feet.

In the kitchen, the dishes were dumped out of the cupboards, half lying smashed on the counters and floor. The fridge lay open, stuff falling out like intestines. The room reeked of spoiled food mingling with air freshener. She went down the hall and the bedroom, study, and bathroom were all just as bad.

"Holy fuck," Zee said, pulling up her magic sight.

Witches had natural abilities besides their elements, usually two or three. The most she'd heard of was six. She had two, teleportation and the ability to see magic. Usually spells faded after a few hours, but these were so thick they'd be here for days.

The remnants of tracking and scrying spells lay over everything like fingerprint dust.

The most prominent color was a teal and purple swirl. Probably the main agent on the case, but for all she knew, one or more of these signatures was from members of the Chaos Kings.

Zee pulled her kit out of her purse and took samples of the spells, locking them in plastic baggies. There were at least half a dozen, a few more that could've been mixes. Whatever went down here, it'd been huge. But battle or just spells to find Jarred, she couldn't be sure.

And if Agents had been here, either trying to capture Jarred or investigating, why didn't it say so in the file?

Zee packed it up and headed back to her store. There wasn't much to be done with the samples until she could get to the witches' database in the main reality, and the best time to get in without detection was at night.

# # #

"Hey, Sampson," Zee said, leaning back in the chair in her inner office. It was a third of the size of the outer office, and just a desk, shelves of files on the magical inventory, and juuuuust enough room to walk between them. "It's Zee."

"Hello, Sarah."

She rolled her eyes. Why did her most useful smuggling friends have to be the two guys in the reality who insisted on using her first name? "Do you know anything about the Chaos Kings?"

"Down to business as always," Sampson said, Irish accent gravely with age.

"You know it. So, anything?"

"Why would I know anything about them?"

"Because you're one of the best smugglers in the reality."

"Flattery will get you everywhere. Just not now. I haven't even been approached by the Kings."

"Really?"

"I will admit I am a bit surprised myself, but yes."

The Kings subcontracted and recruited agents for crying out loud. Why wouldn't they go to the guy with the record for the most smuggling arrests without one conviction?

"Have they come to you?" Sampson asked.

Zee froze. "Um, no."

"Hum."

"I can't believe I didn't think of that. Why haven't they tried hiring me? I'm one of the best smugglers and everyone in the underground knows I'm no fan of the Agency. You, me and James are at the top of the smugglers' list, at least of the people the Agency hasn't locked away. You and I have managed to keep everything looking legal, and James is a vampire that erased all his info from Agency databases and is just too powerful to capture. But they haven't asked any of us. You would think we'd be shoo ins."

"Maybe they thought we wouldn't help since we've never smuggled drugs."

"Nobody ever smuggled drugs before the Kings started last year."

"Good point."

"So you don't know anything?"

"I know what you do. Just the rumors flying around Parata and the Smugglers' Society."

"Have there been any rumors about the Kings trying to recruit out of the Society?"

"Not that I've heard of."

"That's weird, isn't it? We have this not-so-secret society dedicated to smuggling and this gang doesn't think to try to use it?"

"Maybe it's too established for them?"

I frowned. "Maybe."

"Sorry, lass. Tracking criminals is your area. I just am one."

She gave him the chuckle he was looking for. "Thanks anyway."

"Of course."

There was a pause and she heard mumbles.

"Try some vampires in the Society," he said a moment later. "Maybe the Kings would be more keen on using them."

"I already asked James and he's got nothing. Laurel's the next on my list to call, but I'm not so sure. I mean, the Kings've used and paid off agents. They're not exactly afraid of getting up in the Agency's face."

"One moment." More mumbles. "I've got Karen Timber here and she says she hasn't been approached, or heard anything about

85

the Kings in the Society."

"Shit." Karen was the gossip queen of the vamp underground. She was going to be Zee's call after Sampson.

"She says no one in her circle knows anything," Sampson said.

"That takes out most of the vampires in the Society. And those guys are most of the powerful ones."

"Try Laurel?"

"Yeah, she's next. But I think I'm missing something. They aren't hiring the usual suspects. They aren't even trying. Anyway, tell Karen thanks for me."

"Will do. Good-bye, Sarah."

"Bye." She hung up, swearing under her breath. Why would the Kings recruit straight from the Agency, but leave vampires out of it?

She checked the clock. Still too early in the morning to call. Vampires could be awake during the day, and even go out in sunlight, but Laurel wasn't a morning person. Calling before noon wasn't advised.

Zee dialed the familiar number at the university instead.

"Professor Marlow," a stodgy New England accent greeted after a moment.

"Hey Professor. It's Zee."

"How is my favorite delinquent?"

She smiled. Carl Marlow, i.e. Professor, was the head of the Criminal Justice department at the university. He was the one who took Zee in at seventeen, helped her get through the rest of high school, and housed her when she started college. When she got her powers, she told him. Even though witches weren't ever supposed to tell normal people.

"I'm at the beginning of a case and I need some help," she said.

"Tell me."

She gave him the quick version. "So here's my problem. The Kings have been known for about a year, but everything is secondhand. They wipe the memories of everyone who has worked with them... at least the ones who are still alive. The Kings have hired agents, but, and here's the weird thing, they haven't hired any known smugglers or tried selling their stuff at the Smuggler's Society. So, why?"

"Is there anything similar about the agents who were hired?"

"One second." She checked the file. "Different countries, races, genders, backgrou..."

"Ages?"

She paused, reading the specs on the arrested agents. "Huh. They're young. None of them have been agents more than two years and the oldest was twenty-six."

"That's the why. These gang members are obviously intelligent. When they need to subcontract or someone to help them through the Agency's magical borders, they choose people in a position to be helpful, like agents, but make sure to grab ones who aren't experienced enough to pose too much of a threat. If these Kings had hired or tried to blackmail you, what would you have done?"

"Agreed, and set up a sting to catch them."

"Exactly. These Kings don't want to have to worry about being tricked, so they go after pups."

"So I need to look at students and junior agents." This was why she called Professor. He saw things she didn't. "Thank you, Professor."

"Anytime. You're still coming to dinner tonight, right?"

Fuck. She'd completely forgotten about their weekly dinner. "Yeah, I've just got to get a few things done first."

They hung up and she pinched her nose.

Why did she have the feeling it was going to be a long night?

CHAPTER FOUR

Zee focused on her store for the rest of the morning, letting the Jarred problem percolate in the back of her head, and called Laurel after noon.

"Hey, Laurel-leaf."

"Hey, Princess." She sounded fully awake. Good.

"You know I hate that nickname," Zee said.

"Which is why I use it." Laurel was Irish and still had a thick accent. Her and Sampson had been friends since he was a first-year witch. Zee still thought it was weird to look at Laurel and know she'd been in her twenties for a few decades. It'd probably be weirder when Zee was older like Sampson and her vampire friends were still the same.

"Yeah, yeah. Anyway, I was wondering if you've heard anything about the Chaos Kings?"

"Nothing you haven't. Why?"

Zee gave her the quick version.

"Jarred Krentz?" Laurel asked when Zee was done.

"Yes."

"He was at Yuri's club last night."

"What?" Adrenaline buzzed through her blood and she sat up straight. A lead? An actual lead? "Did you see him or did you hear he was there?"

"I saw him. He'd been hiding at Yuri's for the past two days. He said he was falsely accused and on the run. He's trying to prove he's innocent and he had to get out of the reality, without setting off any Agency alerts, to get proof. I helped him get out."

No way is my luck this good. "Which reality?"

She paused. "I can't. Memory potion."

Zee slumped. *Dammit!* "I knew it couldn't be that easy."

"Sorry."

"Did he say anything else? Like what he was on the run for?"

"Nope, said the less I knew, the better. Is he involved with the Kings?"

"Accused of it."

She hissed. "Poor lad. I wish I knew where those bloody bastards were based. I'd rip out all their throats."

"You're not the only one. It's *frustrating*. They're like ghosts. Everyone's heard of them over the past year. We see Chaos Candy on the streets and have agents admitting to being paid off. But nobody knows who the Kings are, where they are, or even how many of them there are. How can they have gotten so big, so fast, without anybody knowing anything?"

"My guess is it's a small group. That the Kings are one or two orders at most. They found Chaos Candy in some other reality, realized the profit potential, and subcontracted as needed with very strict blood contracts written up. They know what they're doing. I wouldn't be surprised if they were agents."

"The sad thing is, neither would I." Zee sighed. "Do you have any way of contacting Jarred?"

"I have his number, and can do a general cross realities spell to get the call out, but if I were him, I wouldn't pick up."

"Me neither, but he might text back. Can you give me the

number?"

"Sure, but…"

"I know he won't pick up, but I can text and see if he'll let me help."

Laurel gave her the number and Zee sent out a text with a reality crossing spell explaining she was on the case and she wanted to help.

Now she just had to wait to hear from him.

After a morning of dead ends and phone calls, she finally had a lead.

# # #

Zee left Penny to close and went to her foster dad's place around sunset.

"Hey, Professor!" she called as she walked in.

He came out of the kitchen with a towel over his arm and she gave him a hug.

"Hello, Zee." He pulled back and held her at arm's length. "I swear, the only time you eat is when you're over here. You're too skinny."

He always said that and she always laughed. Professor was six three and a scarecrow, all long limbs and skin and bone. He had a thick head of greyin... *silvering* black hair, naturally tan skin, warm brown eyes, and a charming smile.

She held up the Riesling and slipped off her shoes. "I've got a few leads and a long night ahead of me."

"Which obviously means Riesling." Professor took it from her and put it in the freezer.

They ate and chatted, catching each other up on the events of the week. It was a nice break from the case.

She should've know it wouldn't last.

Halfway through a dessert of sorbet and Riesling, Zee's phone buzzed against her hip.

"Sorry." She picked it up. Unavailable. A lot of witches' numbers were so there was no reason to think it was Jarred, but her heart rate picked up anyway. "Excuse me."

She walked into the living room and answered.

"Zee here."

"Hello, Little Princess," a voice with a barely detectable east European accent said.

She jerked straight, grabbing the edge of the couch, heart pounding like it was trying to escape through her sternum. Copper coated her tongue and she gulped. That only helped if you had saliva left though.

She hadn't heard that voice in *years*.

The ache echoed through her chest.

They said the first thing you forgot about someone was their voice.

She'd never forgotten his.

"Hello, Kostos," she said. "Can I help you with something?"

"Don't sound so nervous, Zee."

She hadn't heard him say her name in over three years. Parata wasn't big when compared to the real world, but it was big enough to avoid someone if you wanted to. His voice was a low growl and always hinted at violence.

Or other things.

"I merely want to know where Jarred Krentz is," he said.

"Why would I know?"

"Don't be coy. Do you have any leads?"

She sat down, running her free hand over the couch's buttery leather. How did she play this? Keep pretending she didn't know what he was talking about, or go with her tough-as-nails bounty hunter image?

"If I knew where he was, he'd already be in Agency custody," Zee said arrogantly. "And if I had a lead, I wouldn't tell you. Don't insult me, Kostos."

"And stealing our file wasn't insulting?"

"It wasn't meant to be. I was hoping you'd never know you were on the case."

"Why?"

Her lip curled up. "You know why."

"Don't tell me the great Sarah Zeewowski's afraid of me."

"I'm not stupid, Kostos. And the last time we met, you said you'd skin me alive the next opportunity you got. If we're both chasing the same guy and we get in each other's way, then oops, accidents happen, right?"

"I was angry," he said, voice empty and flat as a soda left open overnight.

"Yeah, I've got a couple of scars on my arm and back that can attest to that fact. Nice work, by the way. I still can't figure out how to heal them."

"I thought you were attacking my brother."

"I *was*. The part you're leaving out is he needed attacking. And instead of asking me, trying to assess the situation, you attacked *me*. Kind of sours a friendship."

They'd had this same fight over three years ago. They'd both done what they thought they had to do.

Apparently time didn't change that.

It didn't change a lot of things.

The scars on her body weren't the only ones he'd left.

She shoved the thought down.

"Friendship?" Kostos said. "That's one way of putting it."

Something bubbled in her chest and she shoved it down too.

Emotions didn't have a place in her world.

"I'm only going to say this once, Kostos," she said. "Find a new case. If I see you on this one, I'm going to assume you're trying to make good on your threat, and I'll react with appropriate force."

"Well then," he said, warm threat crept into his voice, the thread-weaver once again, "I'd better make sure you don't see me."

The line went dead.

"Flying shitballs of death!" She smacked the couch and clipped the phone back onto her belt.

Kostos *probably* wouldn't go out of his way to kill her. She'd been trying to take his brother in for a series of rapes and Kostos had just reacted, protecting family before he knew what his brother was accused of.

And once he knew, he had left Zee be.

But still.

She expected a certain amount of risk in her professions,

smuggling and other inter reality activities would put her in the crosshairs of the Agency if they ever found out, and chasing down criminals definitely put her on the shit list of some of the more unsavory characters in their world.

But this was different.

Kostos was a good agent. Straight as a razor. Loyal as a sheepdog. The kind of guy she'd want watching her back if he hadn't already stabbed her in it.

She walked back into the kitchen, shaking off Professor's questions with a smile, saying the call was about the person she was trying to find.

"It's nearly ten o'clock at night," he said.

She shrugged, taking a sip of the wine. What could she say? "I..."

Da, da, daaaa, her phone trilled, indicating a text.

Her heart leaped up her throat and she ripped the phone off her belt. It said unavailable.

Jarred?

She clicked on the text.

"This is above your paygrade. Get that big nose out of our business before we flatten it. Consider this a warning."

A cartoon crown danced on thin legs at the bottom of the message. The Kings? How would they know she was on the case? Why would they care if Jarred really was innocent?

"Ahhhhhhhhhh!" Professor screamed, his chair scratching the floor as he shoved it back.

Zee looked up just in time to see him stumble to his feet.

A Husky's head sat in the middle of the table.

It was severed cleanly near the bottom of the neck, the bottom cauterized so it didn't leak, the thick grey hair neatly brushed. It faced Zee, staring at her with icy blue eyes she'd know anywhere.

It was Sasha.

CHAPTER FIVE

Zee stared into Sasha's cold, dead eyes, rushing filling her ears. Nick gave her to Zee the week after they became an order because she'd told him she hadn't had a pet besides strays who came and went since her parents had been alive. Sasha depending on her was the only thing that got her out of bed for the month after her order died.

Whoever did this made a huge mistake.

They just made it personal.

"Zee," came through the river running over her ears.

She pushed back her chair and stood, every motion slow and precise, like a drunk trying not to fall over.

"Zee?" Professor said again. "Zee!"

She kept staring at Sasha, the dead dog's eyes cold and confused, like the poor girl didn't know what she did wrong.

Nothing. She'd never done anything wrong. She'd been a good dog.

"Sarah Lynn Zeewowski!" Professor appeared in front of her, leaning over and snapping in front of her face. "Snap out of it."

"My dog's dead." She could barely hear her own voice.

"I know, and I'm sorry, but you have to focus. What did that text say?"

"Told me to stay out of it, that this was a warning."

He took her hands. "You're onto something."

"But I'm not." She shook her head.

She was missing something. If she could think, she could figure out what it was.

Zee could still see Sasha out of the corner of her eye. She turned her head those last few degrees away and Professor moved with her.

"Who knows you're working this case?" Professor asked.

"Probably everyone in Parata by now."

"No leads?"

"Nothing besides the one from Laurel, but that's just to find Jarred. Why would the Kings care about warning me off if he's not one of them? And how would they know? Laurel would never tell them."

Professor shook his head and let her go. "I don't know."

There was too much bouncing around in her head, too many questions. They were distractions. She had to push t...

Distractions.

Fuck!

She thrust power out without another thought, making a shield around the room it'd take a nuke to break through. It glowed white and sparkled for a few seconds as it set, the low hum of magic making her teeth vibrate. She sent her magic searching around the house.

Three figures popped up on the magical radar outside.

Something flashed across her vision, knocking her shield out.

"Get down!" she yelled, hitting the floor with Professor two seconds behind her.

The spell flew over their heads, smashing into the wall and supernovaing all over it just as a figure appeared next to the table.

Zee grabbed the figure with telekinesis and threw him into the island counter separating the kitchen from the dining area.

"Umph," the man grunted, flopping to the ground, fully visible. He was nearly as tall and thin as Professor and wore black clothes and a ski mask.

A ski mask? Really?

She was still moving too slow, thinking through molasses. The freeze spell hit her before she realized it and she stopped in place, eyes jerking back and forth as she struggled against the spell.

The man she threw into the counter stood, rubbing his lower back and glaring at her.

He took a step forward.

And his body jerked around, twisting his neck to the side, eyes still locked on her as he fell to the ground dead.

The spell on Zee broke and she shook out her hands, focusing on the witch who froze her.

She drew her power through him, felt his magic swirling through his blood, as real and tangible as blood cells. She grabbed onto the river of power, lit his blood on fire, gripping his heart with her mind.

And squeezed it into a pulp.

His eyes flew wide behind the mask. They were a deep, dark blue. Their light died and he crumbled to the floor.

Zee went limp too, knees kissing wood two seconds later.

No, not yet. Couldn't let go yet.

She focused, trying to see the magics, friend and foe, in the house.

She flew across the room, too fast to teleport herself to safety, and slammed into the wall behind the table, arm flying out to catch her.

Her forearm snapped in half on impact.

The world went red and she didn't feel it as she hit the ground.

"Boss wants her alive," a woman said through the haze of red.

"The human?" another voice said. This one sounded male.

"He can be leverage. Was there another witch or just her?"

The woman screamed, short and shrill and a thump echoed across Zee's ears like a shot.

Zee opened her eyes. She hadn't realized they were closed. The table had been pushed aside and the woman lay dead on the ground.

"What the fuck!" the man yelled. "Who's there?"

Zee grinned, she knew exactly who was watching her back.

For someone who claimed he hated drama, James sure did have a thing for grand entrances.

She blinked, focusing on the arm laying in front of her.

Huh. Some jagged off-white thing stuck an inch out of a ripped, leaky red hole in her forearm. It lay in a sticky pool of bright red liquid.

The last time she donated, the blood was collected in a vial. This was just a waste.

The floor burst into flames in front of her and legs appeared by her head.

"Oh fires," the proper British voice said, "always so

dramatic."

She would've laughed at the hypocrisy if she wasn't numb.

The flames disappeared and the air unzipped across the room. The man jumped through and the slit in reality closed in two seconds.

James kneeled next to her, holding his hands over her. "I am sorry, Sarah, I should have been prepared for him to run. We will track him."

"How?" she asked as his healing magic swept through her, knitting her arm and flushing the pain out in a few seconds.

She sat up, staring at him so she wouldn't look at the table. "They killed my dog."

James' eyes flicked over her shoulder and his mouth stretched into a thin line as he met her eyes.

He knew what Sasha had meant to Zee.

Sasha was family. Two legs or four, you protect your family.

"Professor?" Zee asked.

"Right here," he said after a moment. "I'm okay."

"Good. Can you get somewhere safe for the night?"

"Yeah. I can get a hotel."

"Good. James?"

"We will find this man," James said. "He will tell us where his friends are. We will avenge her, I swear it to you."

She nodded. "You can figure out what reality he went to?"

"I can not guarantee finding him. However, I have an idea."

CHAPTER SIX

James took them through a portal and before Zee could blink, she found herself sitting on a stiff lounge chair.

"Sarah." James kneeled in front of her, resting his hands on her knees and looking her straight in the eyes. "Sarah, please look at me. I have to fetch someone. Will you be all right if I leave you here? Just for a few minutes."

"Where are we?"

"This is called the Inn Between Worlds. It has been here longer than Parata."

"What... I don't understand."

"It is a magical in-between place. It has been sitting between realities since before witches in our world could travel between realities. No one in the Agency knows of it. I barely learned of its existence and connected it to our reality last year."

Zee nodded, not tracking half of what he said.

This couldn't be happening.

Sasha was dead.

Her baby. The creature who'd been with her since she was twenty-one years old.

That dog got her through some of the worst times in her life in the past seven years. Her order, who were closer than family, dying. Professor's cancer scare. The attack by Kostos that left her with permanent scars.

Even the more mundane things like her business struggling were easier with the big fluffball. And now she was gone.

"Sarah," James said, voice as gentle as he used on his

patients.

She could barely focus on his face.

"Sarah," James cupped her cheek, "I need to know you will stay here and you will not do anything rash."

His bright blue eyes made practically every female he turned them on melt but Sarah had always been immune.

He was her friend, one of the best she'd made since she was a kid when making friends was easy, and to think of him as anything other than that made her gag a little.

But she could see why girls fell for him. Those eyes bore into her, commanding her to pay attention and listen.

She nodded.

"Where are you going?" she asked as he stood.

"I am fetching Nathan. I can not think of anyone better equipped to help with this."

She licked her lips and nodded again.

Nathan was one of the only, if not the only, witch who could see the future out of their reality.

Their reality had so much magic, so many potential paths for the future to take, that they were taught seeing the future was impossible.

Except Nathan could to a certain extent.

He could see possibilities, and even sometimes what would lead to them.

And he could see what'd happened as well. Not nearly as rare, but extremely helpful on a case.

"Stay," James said again before disappearing.

Zee looked around.

She was in what looked like a perfectly normal hotel bar.

The long wooden bar gleamed under bright lights and hundreds of bottles lined the wall behind it. The little tables dotting the room were the same beautiful dark wood and had different dark colored cushions with the same intricate gold pattern to make it clear they were the same set.

She stood, stretching her arms far above her head and popping her back before walking to the bar.

The bartender appeared in front of her and she didn't even jerk.

She wasn't feeling much of anything.

She'd like to keep it that way.

"I need a drink," she said, barely able to make her mouth work.

Shock?

Probably.

"Yes, yes, you do," the man said, nodding his head with slow precise movements. "What's your poison?"

She shook her head. "I… ugh, usually wine, maybe some rum, but I want strong and quick. My dog was just murdered."

Pity swamped his face and he turned, grabbing a bottle with golden brown liquid.

"That calls for bourbon, the good stuff," he said, pouring her what she was pretty sure was a triple and sliding it across the smooth top to her.

"Ice?" she asked.

"No. You don't put ice in the good stuff. Maybe some water with good scotch. Just drink this straight. Trust me. Sip it, don't shoot."

He poured himself a shot and held the glass up. She followed suit.

"To absent companions," he said, tapping her glass and taking a long sip.

She took a drink and for a second thought her taste buds were as numb as the rest of her as the expected burn was barely a tickle.

She took another sip, tasting it more, detecting the sweet caramel and vanilla as it poured over her tongue.

No, it wasn't her tongue, it was the drink. It really was just that smooth.

She downed the drink a little too fast considering how good it was and tapped the counter for another.

She glanced up as the bartender poured another drink and a bronze statue of a husky appeared over the mirror stretching from near the ceiling to below her line of sight.

The husky sat, staring straight ahead with watchful eyes.

Watching for danger as all good dogs do.

# # #

"Sarah?"

The voice made Zee jump and she tried to get her bourbon glazed eyes to focus as she turned her head.

James sat on the stool next to her and she giggled.

The prim and proper Dr. James Morganson sitting on a stool with his expensive loafers dangling in midair made a sight.

She laughed harder.

"Samuel," James said, turning his gaze to the bartender, "how much have you given her?"

Sam shook his head. "Told ya before, Morganson, it's Sam. And it's not short for Samuel."

James narrowed his eyes and Zee giggled again.

James had a thing about only using full names. Not knowing someone's full one bugged him to no end.

And on too many ounces of bourbon to count, it was fucking hilarious.

Zee bent over the bar, laughing so hard tears leaked out.

Or maybe that had nothing to do with the laughter.

The thought sobered her and she coughed as she lifted her head.

James had changed out of his three-piece suit to black slacks and a blue button down. That was about as casual as he got. She'd crashed at his place before and even his PJs were fancy satiny things she didn't think anyone wore outside of movies.

"Sarah," James said, taking away her latest half full glass, "you need to stop drinking and sober. We have work to do."

"Where's Natey? Can't start without him," she said, pretty sure she was slurring as she reached for her drink.

James flicked a finger and her glass disappeared.

"You are a controlling *asshole*," she said, pounding on the counter. "Where's Nate?"

"Nathan is using the facilities and will be here momentarily. Mr. Bartender, would you mind serving her something to sober her, and a Gatorade?"

She snorted.

He couldn't bring himself to call the man Sam so he made up a name basically.

"What is it with you and the full names thing?" Zee asked.

James sighed, meeting her eyes.

"Names have power, my dear. You label your enemies. You label your friends. These help you define and therefore exert control over your world."

"So you insist on using my given name because you're a controlling ass? It makes perfect sense now."

"Your argument is flawed."

"Yeah, well, I'm drunk."

"Which brings us back to what started this ridiculous discussion. Stop drinking, Sarah. It is not helping you."

"And we're back to you being a controlling ass."

"I give up."

"Finally."

"Sarah, you are a horrible drunk, and you know this."

A glass full of something she could tell was magical appeared on the bar and Sam turned and pulled a Gatorade out of the little fridge on the far side.

"I will take care of her bill," James said.

"I buy my own drinks," Zee said with a sneer, taking the sobering concoction and downing it in one shot.

Her head and vision cleared almost instantly and she grabbed the Gatorade and chugged.

Based on past experiences with sobering potions, if she didn't hydrate fast, she'd be in serious pain in about one minute.

James looked at her and handed a strange looking card to the bartender. "You do not know what currency they take here. And a grieving lady should not pay for her own drinks."

"Sexist," a jovial voice said from behind.

"Nathan!" she said, slamming down the drink and swiveling around.

Nathan was only nineteen when he was turned and could pass for a high schooler easily too when he was clean shaven. But for now, he'd grown out his blond beard enough to look manly and had his just as naturally blond hair cut and professionally styled. He wore jeans and cowboy boots to go with the Texan accent but had a designer rugged guy plaid shirt on that said he never got closer to cows than a cheeseburger.

Nathan leaned forward and hugged her tight, half lifting her off the stool and setting her on her feet.

He wasn't much more than an inch or two taller than her, short for a guy, but he made up for it with enough trips to the gym to keep himself thick with muscle.

"Hey girl," he said, staring into her eyes as she pulled back. "I'd ask how you are, but I can see the pain. I am so sorry. I know how much Sasha meant to you."

"Yeah," Zee said, grabbing the Gatorade and taking a long gulp. "I… can't talk about that." She took another long drink. "Where to?"

"Down to business. I can respect that," Nathan said. "Ol' blue eyes here said the guy ran to another reality without a trace, right?"

James clenched his jaw at the nickname but nodded anyway.

"So we go there first and I try to get a vision," Nathan said. "And step one is done. See, I'm helping already."

Zee looked between him and James.

"We stopped by the house," James said. "Nathan has already tracked the man to the next reality."

"Oh," Zee said. "Good. I thought that'd take longer. Let's go!"

"Waiting on you, sweetheart," Nathan said.

She toasted him with her bottle of Gatorade before tossing back the rest of it. "I'm ready."

James nodded at Sam and led them through the doorway into a sweeping grand hall reminiscent of old timey southern mansions.

"You said this was an in-between," Zee said as James started up the stairs. "What does that mean?"

"It means this inn sits outside of natural realities. It is a created one, much like Parata. However, instead of being a bubble off of a main reality, it is a reality in of itself, and it is not tied to any one reality. It connects to thousands of them, possibly more, with no explanation of who made it or how it manages that level of magic without imploding. It is a mystery; however, it is an extremely useful one."

They hit the top of the stairs and the hall stretched far on both sides, hundreds of doors with no numbers but different names, paintings and markings on them.

"How do you tell where we need to go?" Zee asked.

"Focus on the reality we want, and the inn will take us to the door," James said. "It is really quite extraordinary."

"Quite," Zee said with no small amount of mocking as her stomach lurched and Sasha's face appeared in her head.

She shoved the memory down.

It was good to be sober for a hunt, but she wasn't exactly thrilled about having to feel again.

Still, the goal kept the emotions at bay.

Find man, capture man, torture him into spilling where the Kings' headquarters were, kill him after torturing him for a little longer for fun, then go into the headquarters and do it all again.

Lather, rinse, repeat.

Zee took a deep breath as James and Nathan each took a hand.

"Do not say it," James said.

"Say what?" she asked.

"Whatever crude joke you were about to make about being in between two men."

"I actually wasn't going to make a joke. Not in a joking mood."

"Oh, I am terribly sorry, Sarah. I should not scold you so. You are usually…"

"Yeah, I know. Do your thing. I'm sure I'll get the sense of humor back."

No, she was pretty sure it'd died with her dog, but it seemed like something the old Zee would say.

James squeezed her hand and focused his laser gaze on the hall.

The hall sped around them, almost like the doors were a dial being twirled, and snapped to a stop without warning.

Zee's stomach lurched and she doubled over as Nathan wobbled around next to her.

"I apologize," James said. "The first time can be quite unnerving."

"No need to tell me that. That's how it goes with me and first times," Zee said, not really feeling the joke.

James didn't even shoot her a glare, just rubbed her arm before letting her go and opening the door.

A wave of dry, hot air hit Zee and she sniffed, backing away.

"It feels like home during the summer," Zee said.

"It appears to be close," James said. "Southern Utah. One of the national parks, I believe."

"What reality?" Nathan asked.

"I am not sure it has a name," James said. "The coordinates seem familiar, but I can not for the life of me remember from where I heard them."

"And we're sure he's in Southern Utah in this reality?" Zee asked.

"No," Nathan said. "We just know that's where he went. We'll have to track once we're in there."

"Shall we?" James asked, lips drawn tight.

"This feels like a trap," she said.

"I do not believe it is. The man is running. And has a good reason to be afraid."

"Yes, you're terrifying. Good for you." Zee rolled her eyes and pulled out her gun and one of her knives.

Just in case.

They walked out into the desert, the night not cooling it much. A giant arch stretched above their heads just to the south and the giggles of night hikers rang across the empty land, nothing to keep the noise from traveling far over the sands.

"Arches," Zee said, almost smiling. "I love this place. Not during the summer because *damn*, but it's my favorite national park. I come here every fall. Sasha can't…"

She slammed her mouth shut and looked down, instant tears clogging her voice.

Sasha couldn't take the desert heat during the summer so they'd come during the fall and sometimes even then would only hike at night.

"Sarah," James said, hugging her to his side.

She shook him off. "Nope. I can fall apart later. Got a guy to find."

James nodded. "Nathan?"

The psychic lifted his hands to the air and tilted his head back, closing his eyes as he muttered to the wind.

Zee could practically hear James thinking how dramatic Nathan was.

"This way," Nathan said after a moment.

Zee and James followed him away from the giant arch and off the trail.

"Just tell me you can get us back," Zee said.

"You never gone off trail, girl?" Nathan asked.

"Yes. In *our* reality. I don't even know if the spells I know will work here. I didn't think to put a magic preserving spell on me before we left to make sure I kept my powers even if the reality isn't magical."

"This world has magic," James said. "Very little of it, though. And do not worry. I cast the spell to bind our powers to us through realities."

"Thanks. Nathan, where the fuck are we going?"

"Patience," Nathan said as James flinched. "There is no rushing perfection."

She wrapped her arms around herself and stared at Nathan as he paused.

He finally moved, jerking so suddenly Zee hopped in place. He twisted complicated symbols in the air, his reality cutting crystal appearing in his hand as he swiped down and cut a hole through the reality.

"Through here," Nathan said. "He left maybe five minutes ago."

"Do you recognize the coordinates?" James asked.

"Yep. Gort reality."

"That's where they get some of the main ingredients for Chaos Candy," Zee said.

"Could be their headquarters, but why go right there if he knows we're following?" Nathan asked.

"Because if that is where his compatriots are, *that* is where he would lay a trap," James said. "We must hurry."

"Hurry into the trap?" Zee asked.

"They will not have as much time to set one up."

"But the guy's had an hour. What was he doing that whole time?" Nathan asked.

"That is an excellent point," James said.

"So he could've gone there to set up from here, then came back here to wait for us and lead us there," Zee said. "Most witches can detect a normal portal within a few minutes, and they don't know we have Nathan, so if they wanted us to follow, they'd have to make sure they left a portal within a few minutes of us. I can see it."

"As can I," James said. "One moment."

Zee felt air charge as James worked a spell and her ears popped as he drew something in the air.

"We are now invisible to all but each other," James said.

"That going to keep them from detecting us?" Nathan asked.

"I included all the usual extras to keep us from being perceived in general," James said.

"Good enough for me," Zee said. "But can they see the reality rip?"

"No," James said.

"Okay. Once more unto the breach." She adjusted her grip on her gun and knife and stepped through after the guys, zipping the portal shut behind them.

The world was a green, lush landscape surrounding one stretch of road under street lights, the exact opposite of the desert. The road turned into a dock stretching out onto a lake. A bar sat at the end of the dock, hanging out over the lake.

Bouncing live country music came from the bar and ducks waddled around the bank sloping into the lake. They probably swam right under the patio of the bar, quacking for patrons to toss them snacks.

"If this is where they have their headquarters," Nathan said, "I'm sorry, but we can't destroy it. I already love this place."

"Yes, you would," James said, face passive except for a slight pursing of the lips.

"Mister proper and classic have a problem with a country bar?" Zee asked.

"I am not a fan of this kind of music, no," James said. "Nathan, the gentleman we are chasing?"

"Yes, right away, sir," Nathan said in a horrible and hilarious British accent.

Nathan closed his eyes and started his thing and Zee looked around.

To the side and a little behind them was a giant parking lot. Not terribly packed, probably not surprising for a weekday night, but not a bad crowd.

"I don't see them setting up shop here," Zee said.

"Neither do I," James said. "However, this does look fairly remote. There could be buildings hiding beyond the trees surrounding this area."

"Yeah."

But something felt off.

"Now, why am I not surprised," came out of the dark.

Zee jumped, pulling her gun up before remembering no one could see them, heart pounding so loud in her skull it gave her a headache.

Kostos appeared out of the air, a blond woman close behind.

He was as big and intimidating as she remembered. About six-foot-four, with buzzed short black hair, naturally tan skin,

115

thick lips and big brown eyes hidden behind surprisingly proper looking small glasses. He was a high school science teacher at a fancy private school in California while in the human world and his nice suits and glasses were the only things scholarly about him.

The rest was raw, caveman.

Zee's body flooded with the urge to run or fight and her legs shook as she took a deep breath, trying to ignore the twinge of her scars.

And the urge to run up and hug him and see how he was at the same time.

"She's here," Kostos said.

"Zee's good," the woman, Zee thought her name might have been Rachel, said, "but even she can't travel through realities without leaving some trail. There's no way anyone from our reality came here without leaving a trail."

Zee snorted.

There were actually a few ways to do it, and now she could add on the inn James had led them through.

"She's here," Kostos said. "I can feel it."

"Hey," Rachel said, stroking his arm, "it's okay. We'll find him. We will find these bastards and put an end to all of this. But you have got to stop obsessing about Zee. She's trying to do her job, just like you. She's not the enemy. She's not working with these guys. She's trying to stop them. Okay?"

She took his chin, forcing it down so he looked her in the eyes. "Okay?"

He took a deep breath and kissed her and they disappeared.

Something zinged through Zee and she clenched her fists.

She hadn't known he was seeing someone in his order.

Not that she *got* to be jealous. They'd left that part of their relationship far behind when she went after his brother, and hadn't been screwing around for a while before that since she'd had a boyfriend at the time.

But still.

"Sarah?" James asked. "Is there something we should be aware of?"

"Those are the agents on the case, or at least two of them," she said, voice steady.

"Sarah, I may not be an empath, and you may hide your expressions well, but there was most certainly a reaction when he kissed her."

"Ancient history, James."

"So you two were intimate at one point?"

"Intimate? What are you, a hundred?"

"Approximately. And you are evasive."

"We screwed around in school… and after school, basically whenever we were both free we'd booty call the other. And then the thing with his brother, and well, this." She jerked a thumb back towards her burn scars.

"Ah. Will this affect your work on this case?"

"Of course not. Why would it?"

He shot her a look.

"It's called casual sex, James, you should try it sometime."

"There is no such thing as something so intimate being

casual. That is an invention of the modern media, pushed no doubt by cads who wish to convince women to sleep with them with no repercussions. No, thank you."

"You're just repressed."

"And you, my dear, are lying to yourself. If the relations were casual, you would not have reacted as you just did. Saying intimacy is casual does not make it so, and you, Sarah, are jealous, and I suspect hurt."

She stared straight forward.

"If you two are done making out over there," Nathan said, opening his eyes and dropping his arms, "bad guys are thataway." He pointed towards the parking lot.

They walked across the lot, Zee looking around the whole time.

Nothing out of the ordinary.

"I've got a bad feeling about this, boys," Zee said.

"Me too," Nathan said as they hit the edge of the parking lot, nothing but dense trees beyond it.

"We are shielded," James said. "It would require a great deal of power to break my charms."

"I feel like this is where Zee should be making a dirty joke," Nathan said, looking at her.

"My funny bone is broken," she said. "And yes, pretty sure there's a dirty joke in there about a broken *bone* too."

James stepped up onto the hard-packed dirt surrounding the parking lot and Zee and Nathan followed, diving into the trees.

"He has no sense of humor today," Zee said.

"He has no sense of humor any day," Nathan said.

"I can hear you," James said.

Zee and Nathan shared a look and she almost smiled as he wiggled his eyebrows.

They slogged forward, the trees seemingly unending.

A scream shattered the night and the trio ran forward, splitting up to barrel through the trees.

The guys disappeared as the ground sloped up, longer legs and the increased vampire strength giving them an advantage.

Zee poured on the speed, keeping a good grip on her gun and knife as someone screamed.

She cleared the slope and ran straight into a rip in reality.

CHAPTER SEVEN

Zee slammed on the brakes too late as the world switched from one forest to another and she crashed into short bushes clustered in front of a giant marble wall.

She clenched her jaw as she fell, training keeping her from screaming in surprise as she half landed on the bushes. She pushed off, scrambling back to her feet, gun still in hand but knife lost to the wilderness.

"Sarah, down!" James yelled from somewhere and she hit the deck, pulling her gun up and looking around with quick, practiced eyes.

The underbrush and trees were thicker here than in the other reality next to the bar, more wild. Something crawled over her arm and she didn't twitch for fear of attracting attention of whatever James was shouting about.

Weren't they still invisible?

Flames shot towards her and she raised a shield just in time as they crashed over her.

So that'd be a no on the invisibility thing.

Zee pulled up her sight and focused on the magic. It was a shimmering gold with black sparkles, and something teal flashed just to the side a split second later.

She smacked the flames down and pushed to her feet.

Where the hell were the guys? Or the attackers?

Even with her sight, all she saw was forest.

"James? Nathan?" she screamed.

Nothing.

"Fuck!"

If whatever this was was enough to take out James and a freaking psychic, what chance did she have?

A figure in a black mask jumped through the rip and Zee shot him dead center without thinking. The bullet ricocheted off a shield an inch away from the man's chest and she shot two more times just in case and threw a fireball, focusing everything on the man.

She felt the shield crack under her pressure just as two more of the masked assholes burst through the rip.

Followed by another asshole, just not masked.

"Zee, how's tricks?" Kostos said, running up to her and wrapping them in a shield.

She dropped her efforts with a sigh.

Shields had never been her strong suit.

Zee stared up at her rescuer as he twisted his hands in the air, making the shield stronger than a cold war bunker.

He dropped his hands and met her eyes.

If she wasn't so doped up on adrenaline already, she was pretty sure that one look would have her heart racing all by itself.

"Threatening me then saving me," she said. "You are a complicated man."

He shrugged. "Hello to you too. Long time no try to kill you."

"Well, I'd say get in line, but these guys will probably get you first," she said.

"I can't believe you're holding a party and forgot to invite me," Kostos said, grin wide and vicious as he raised his arms, and winds grabbed the three and slammed them together.

121

They bounced off each other, shields firmly back in place, and scattered as a handful of them poured through the rip.

"No, I didn't," she said, grinning too as his energy got to her, "but last time I invited you to one, you tried to arrest me… and then kill me."

"I was surprised, I didn't expect you to get out of the magic binding handcuffs."

"Oh please, you've seen me get out of handcuffs, and *that* time I'd consented to being put in them."

"Who carries lockpicks on them to a booty call?"

"They're like guns. You never know when you're going to need them."

"I've got the shield and ripping down theirs if you go on the offense," he said, pulling a flask from his jacket, accent as thick and rough as when she first met him, eyes glowing with the thrill of the fight.

"Just like old times," she said as he downed the flask, emerald and white magic glowing so bright out of it she was surprised the potion didn't melt the metal.

"That power boost for just you, or can anyone ride?" she asked.

"Not calibrated," he said, tossing it to her. "Powerful stuff, so pace yourself."

"I never do," she took a long gulp and screwed back on the cap, jerking as Kostos' earth magic rushed through her system, kicking her powers into overdrive.

Power ripped out of Kostos hard enough to make Zee's teeth ache and her hands drop the flask and she focused on the air, watching the green swirl as his power slammed into the shields around the forming horde.

The moment the first shield broke, she started shooting.

They had backups for power failures, but the first thing most witches did with shields was put up blocks for magic, then they'd get the physical ones back up.

Bullets traveled faster than that.

The first one she hit in the chest and he went down without a sound, the next in the shoulder and that one let out a high-pitched scream that told her it was a woman, the next dodged and barely got grazed on the arm.

Then the shield was back up.

"You know who they are?" Kostos asked, taking a deep breath Zee could feel in her stomach.

"Besides Chaos Kings? Nope," she said. "Will if we can get samples of those magics and you get me into the Agency's database."

"Got anything bigger than those?"

He let another wave lose and she said "Nope," as the magic flew, focusing her eyes and shooting at the gathered mass as the wave crashed through them.

She got a few more before her gun clicked empty, no clue if they were kills, injures or annoyances, as the healthy swarmed by the front lines.

"They're getting over their surprise real fast," she said, slamming her spare mag into the gun as she felt Kostos gathering his energy. She only had those nine bullets left and then her backup gun with eight.

And this was a hell of a lot more than the two orders Laurel had predicted.

Who the fuck were these guys?

"We need to do something more permanent," Zee said.

"Only ten of them," he said. "At least half injured."

"And two of us, and my two friends are missing," she said. "And I don't think I killed any so those injured are going to be healed real fucking fast."

"I'm open to ideas, princess."

"Where's your order?"

"Three working the case in our reality. Rachel went back to report. We were surprised we even found anything."

"How did you figure out we were here?"

"Rip's here. Pretty obvious."

"Any way to call for backup?" she asked.

"Not while I'm holding these guys off."

"Change it up. I block, you blast. One good hard one should do it."

"That's what you always said." He grinned and she didn't bother shooting him a glare.

"On the count of three, we switch, do it fast," she said.

"Again, that's wh-"

"Yeah, I got it, we used to screw and you're joking about it now because you deal with stress by saying stupid shit. I get it, you *jackass*. One, two, three!"

She pulled up her shield as his fell and forced her way through their shields, pushing them down with sheer willpower she knew she'd pay for later as all her magic went into it.

124

Blood sprang from her nose as a headache built behind her eyes and Kostos released the gathering energy in a giant ball of nuclear force air slamming down on the mass of masked attackers.

Zee saw their lifeforces get snuffed out like flames as the supercharged air pancaked the entire crowd.

She dropped her magic, turning her sight off, and turned to Kostos.

"Damn, Zee," he said, muttering something in his original Serbian language before his eyes rolled up and he passed out.

#   #   #

Zee picked up the flask and took a gulp to recharge, then poured the bit left into Kostos' mouth.

But he didn't wake up.

She checked through the flattened mass of bad guys, but they were so damaged by the equivalent of a building being dropped on them that she couldn't tell if she knew any of them or not. She took samples of the magic traces left from the battle and got away from the mess.

She'd never been squeamish, but that was too much for even her.

She dragged the giant pain in the ass through the rip in reality and rested at the top of the hill, about ten feet away from the gash in the air that wasn't closing.

Without Nathan there or access to the Agency computers to look up coordinates, she couldn't even tell what reality this one opened into.

No matter what reality it was though, that kind of tear had to be closed before the realities' energies started bleeding into each other, and especially before anyone saw it and decided to wander through.

That's how Alice got to Wonderland and it was a miracle the only bad thing to come out of it and into their reality was a weird ass children's book.

She was near drained even with the potion's help, Kostos was down, James and Nathan were missing, and all their potential leads were dead.

If James and Nathan weren't here, they were either being held captive or dead.

And there wasn't much out there that could hold James Morganson against his will, let alone when he had his psychic sidekick along.

She didn't feel anything as she pulled out her reality slicing crystal.

More friends dead, more to make the Kings pay for once she found them.

More to drink away once this was all over.

If she survived.

"Wait," Kostos crooked out of nowhere.

She didn't even flinch, too numb for surprise, and glanced at him.

"Got to figure out where they came from," Kostos said, still lying flat on his back in the grass. "We can follow them, but gotta do it fast."

He rolled over, coughing.

"We've got no backup and practically no powers," Zee said. "What do we do if we find them?"

"Fight."

"Not drained like this. We regroup and we come back."

"The trail will fade by then. I can track it, but it's got to be fast."

"You got any more of those powerup potions?"

"As a matter of fact," he said, pulling another flask from his belt under his untucked shirt. "Ladies first. And it's going to hurt."

"Promises, promises," Zee said, taking the flask and downing a giant gulp before she could think about it.

Fire burned down her esophagus like liquified chili powder and she gagged as she fell to the ground, barely managing to keep the flask upright.

Kostos half lunged, half scooted forward and took the flask from her hand.

She nodded her thanks as she curled up into a ball and the fire spread.

It flowed down her extremities like burning wicks through them and sparked at the fingertips, finally dulling after seconds that lasted a lifetime, and she took a deep breath.

It was the Agency's basic potion and not Kostos' own version like the last one they took. She remembered the feel of it. It increased the natural magic, like getting an IV, but the unnatural growth was interpreted by the body as pain and it took a lot of effort to dull the effects.

Witches added everything from painkiller spells to extra ingredients to actually stop it from hurting in the first place to their own versions, but sometimes the basic stuff had to do.

Kostos was clenched up in pain as she pushed to her feet and he relaxed as she looked around.

The rip was still open. It was only a matter of time before someone wandered by. They weren't *that* far from the parking lot.

"Do you know how to close that?" she asked. "It's not a normal, opened by crystal portal."

"If it's not one of our portals, no," he said.

"I do," a voice behind made Zee jump and turn.

James stood not ten feet away, straightening his cuffs with pursed lips.

His shirt was ripped across the chest like someone took a swipe with a sword and his normally perfectly groomed hair stuck out every which way, but he looked fine besides that.

Zee pressed her hands over her face, rocking back on her heels before running forward and half jumping on James as she hugged him.

He squeezed her back. "It takes far more than an ambush to destroy me, Sarah," he whispered into her hair.

"Thank god, I can't have any more friends dying on me."

She let him go and punched his arm.

"Sarah!" James yelped.

"Don't scare me like that!" she said. "Nathan?"

"He is already on the other side of this hill, tracking where those attackers came from."

She sighed. "What happened to you two?"

"We were ambushed and taken to some other pocket reality.

Some sort of holding cell that disabled the reality crystals, similar to the Agency's cells. Silly creatures did not dare search me, and well, it is very difficult to hold a man when he has more than one way to travel through realities."

She grinned.

"Lead the way, ol' blue eyes."

He pointed at her. "No, do not start that as well."

# # #

"Anything?" Zee asked after they'd been waiting in the next reality for Nathan to track the bad guys from there.

Nathan shook his head. "There's something, but it just goes back to our reality."

"Maybe that's where they came from," Kostos said.

"Hiding in plain sight? Right under the Agency's nose?" Nathan nodded. "Could be."

"I've got to get my samples into the Agency records anyway," Zee said. "Something about this is really bugging me. I want to know who some of these were."

James made a noise and she glanced at him. He shook his head, flicking his eyes towards Kostos.

"Kostos," Zee said, "can you get us into the records, *without* being detected?"

"It's my badge if we get caught," he said.

"It's our lives if we do," Nathan said, pointing his finger between himself and James.

"Then we don't get caught," Zee said.

# # #

"Nathan, you okay with guard duty?" Zee asked as they crouched in the underbrush just outside the parking lot.

The Agency's California headquarters was based just outside of San Diego, hidden on a military base. They got onto the base easily enough with magic and invisibility spells, but the Agency building would have some real security.

"Not really," Nathan said. "I have a bad feeling."

"Vision?" she whispered. Not because they were audible to the human's prowling the base, because she didn't want Kostos to know.

"No," he said. "Those are harder in this reality. But it's a feeling. And mine are usually right."

"That's why we need you watching our backs," she said. "Please."

He opened his mouth and James said, "Nathan, you are the best equipped to be on watch. You are staying here."

Nathan snapped his mouth shut but didn't look happy about it as he parked himself next to the door and vanished with a seamless spell.

Kostos placed his hand on the metal door and it vanished.

Zee and James followed him into the dark hall, neither so much as flinching as the door snapped back into existence, leaving them in near darkness, the only light a slight glow along the walls.

Zee cleared her throat and James said, "You may speak. I have us under a shield."

"Same kind of shield the Kings got through?" Kostos asked.

"Better," James clipped off with a tone so icy it could freeze off a dick. "Even so, nothing short of an Agency level spell breaker should have been able to breach that shield. These are no mere street criminals."

"They have been using agents," Zee said, keeping her voice low no matter what James said about his shield. "Maybe they got a spell at that level from one of them."

"Where did you hear they've been using agents?" Kostos asked as he opened a door on the right.

"Everywhere," Zee said. "It's pretty common knowledge in criminal circles. Agents seem to know about it too."

"Yeah, it's not supposed to be out that a ton of agents have been caught working for them, or died fighting them." Kostos turned on the lights and shut the door behind them.

The place looked the same as it had back when Zee had been an agent. Half the room taken up by a giant server, the air buzzing with the fans to keep it cool, and laptops and plain wooden tables in the other half.

Zee loaded the samples of magic in her bag into the computer and set it to searching. Considering the size of the database, it could take a minute or a day to find them all. It just depended how long it took to find each match.

Zee took a seat at the table farthest from the door with her back to the wall so she could see and had time to react if anyone showed up. The guys took either side of her and she mentally rolled her eyes.

"We each take a different database and run searches, print off anything that looks relevant?" Zee asked.

"Sounds good," Kostos said.

"Exactly what I was thinking," James said.

Kostos got them into the server and each of them started digging through files, looking for any mention of drugs, the Chaos Kings, or smuggling.

#   #   #

"What do we have then?" Zee asked after forever and a half, standing up and stretching before kneeling on the ground to spread out the pages they'd printed.

They'd switched to putting the pages on the floor after the first hour when they ran out of space at the table.

"What don't we have?" Kostos asked.

"Well, I can see if there's anything on the magical signatures yet," Zee said, walking across the room to where she shoved the samples in.

One came back as Kostos and another as Rachel Montoya, the woman in his order, another was too garbled for the computer to read it for a match, and the rest were still being processed.

Zee walked back to the guys. "Only ones so far are you and your girlfriend's."

"We showed up first?" Kostos asked. "Both of us? That's weird."

"Program could've already had you loaded up for some reason."

"Only if we were suspected of a crime."

"Well, I wouldn't put it past you." Zee smiled.

"If you two are quite finished," James said, getting up to look at the mass of papers.

"I have been attempting to maintain some semblance of order. This pile is the agents killed by the Chaos Kings." He pointed then moved over to the next scramble of papers that sort of resembled a pile. "These are the tests performed on the dead and on suspected batches of the drug." And to the next. "These are suspected Chaos King members and agents associated with them." He got up and walked around the circle of papers to indicate the big pile on the other side. "These are the more miscellaneous items."

"Okay," Zee said, looking over at Kostos as she kneeled. "Hey you, want to get down here and look at all this with us? We should be able to put something together with all this."

Kostos grunted and rubbed his forehead, but got up and joined them.

"Try to organize chronologically?" she asked. "I'm not sure what I'm looking for but…"

James nodded. "I concur. I believe seeing things as they have happened would be quite useful. There is a pattern to this madness. I can not quite place it yet, but there is something here."

"I've been trying to keep my stuff at least in a sort of chronological order," Zee said. "So at least there should be some bunches in order in these. When was the oldest one?"

"Over two years ago," James said. "Those were the first killed."

"First killed was the first sighting of the Chaos Kings?" Zee asked. "Or was the connection made later?"

"Later, I believe."

# # #

They pieced together a long line of papers over the next hour, reading as they went to try to get a sense of how things progressed.

133

"So we had our first dead spring two years ago," Zee said, pointing as she inched to the side on her knees. "Next agent gets killed over six months later. They pick up after that, but why such a long gap? And what made them connect that first agent to this all? I don't remember seeing anything like that."

"Nor do I," James said.

"There wasn't," Kostos said. "I've been looking for that since the beginning. They just connected him to the deaths of the others later."

"Okay, and when did the name Chaos Kings first come up?" Zee asked. "It wasn't till, what, about a year ago?"

"Yes," James said, walking down the line of papers to that point in time. "The name was first heard when an agent who was coerced into working with them said that was what they were referring to themselves as."

"Who?" Kostos asked.

"Charles Guard," Zee read off the transcript of his interrogation. "Nothing extraordinary about him. I got his CV online and he was a computer scientist in the human world, only two years out of grad school. I'm assuming he did something with computers for the Agency."

"Assuming?" James asked.

"Yeah. I couldn't find any of his records in the system."

"No way," Kostos said, jumping back to his laptop and typing furiously. "He's got to have a Parata work history somewhere."

"I do this for a living," Zee said. "He doesn't. I can't even figure out what happened to him after this interrogation. He or the Kings wiped it. Maybe that's what they used him for, was to wipe stuff, and after he was caught, they pulled in someone else."

Kostos' eyes flew over the screen. "No…" He said something in Serbian. "Look at this."

Zee and James hurried over and she skimmed the article title over his shoulder.

"It's an article he wrote in college for the school paper. I don't get it."

"Yeah, an article he wrote on using the internet to subvert propaganda by spreading your version of the truth. I remember reading this exact same article here in Parata five years ago."

James shot him a look as Zee rolled her eyes. "He has a photographic memory."

"Eidetic," Kostos said. "I couldn't place his name until I saw this a moment ago, but this was in the Parata paper too. He said something about tweaking it for the magical audience in the article's introduction, but other than small differences, this is the article I read."

"So?" Zee asked.

"So, it's missing. There is no record of this article in the Parata records. This is normal human internet because the search for that man in the Parata servers turned up nothing except that memo."

"He has been erased," James said. "Nearly impossible in this day and age."

"You've done it," Kostos said.

"Yes, and it took extraordinary lengths to do so," James said, forehead creasing. "Sarah, choose another name from the dead."

She grabbed one of the people with the black mark they used to indicate dead from a few months ago. "Wendy Hollinger. Killed by a Chaos Candy overdose in February."

Kostos and James both typed furiously, eyes jerking over their screens as Zee walked behind them.

Both had searches on multiple databases in the Parata servers and were searching the internet while those went.

Zee jumped on her computer and searched the net too, finding the usual smattering of info on all people with that name.

"Obituary," James said after a moment. "In a Wisconsin paper. She was twenty-five and died in a car crash according to this."

"Not unusual for the Agency to make up a story when one of ours dies by magical means," Zee said.

"Yes, however, there is usually a corresponding obituary in the Parata papers. There is none for this woman. She does have a history coming up on the server, however, there is no record of her death."

"I have the same thing," Kostos said. "She became a witch at twenty, her and her order all became teachers at the University after graduating. They met and formed a bonded order while in a teaching program in the real world, so that explains it. Give me a second to look up her order."

His fingers flew and he paused after a moment and Zee got up to look over his shoulder as folders with the names associated popped up.

"She was the fire. The water died first year in an accident on a trip to an alternate reality."

"I remember that," Zee said. "They lost like twenty kids on that trip. It was a huge scandal."

"Yeah, and I don't think Wendy got over it. She'd brought a lawsuit against the Agency for wrongful death, claiming they'd

136

been careless taking students into a war zone. It'd been tied up in court before she died."

"Anyone else in the lawsuit?" Zee asked.

"Yes," James said. "I have it right here." He pointed to the screen.

Zee ran back around the desk to the piles of papers. "I'm going to start reading off names of the dead. You tell me if any of them are on the lawsuit."

Zee ran through only half the names and they already had three other hits.

"And we all know Corbin Madison," Zee said, holding up his folder. "I voted for him for President in the last election."

"He died in the human world," Kostos said. "Magical showdown when his girlfriend's husband came home and found them in bed. Him and the wife were killed and then the husband committed suicide when he saw what he did."

"That's the story," Zee said. "I've got his whole life, resume, and how he died. Everything on the up and up, the guy that killed him and the woman they fought over dead. The coroner's reports on all three confirming it."

She stared at them.

"So why did his name come up in our search?" James asked quietly.

She stood up, nodding.

"Guys, I'm thinking we need to move it on out of here," Zee said. "We take all this with us and finish going through it in a safer location. James?"

He nodded. "I believe my home would be the most secure,

137

yes."

She was actually thinking the inn, but he may not have wanted an agent to know about that.

Especially with what they were piecing together.

"You can't think…" Kostos whispered. "No."

"We've got a bunch of dead people, and the first few we looked into were doing something the Agency didn't like, ran against the president in the last election, or were giving people ideas," Zee said. "Two's a coincidence. Three's a pattern. We need to get out of here, with all this as evidence."

"You can't be suggesting t-"

"No," Zee said, "I'm *saying* it. The Kings aren't killing people or making them disappear. The Agency is."

# # #

"You have your own reality?" Kostos asked as they walked through the slit in the air into James' living room.

"It is a very good way to avert the Agency," James said. "This knowledge does not leave this group."

"Affirmative," Kostos said.

"James, do you have any way of running samples?" Zee asked.

Zee had had to pull her samples out before anything else came up with the scan while the guys gathered the papers.

"No," James said. "I am sorry, Sarah, but even I do not have access to the Agency database."

"I think I can get something off them," Nathan said, holding his hand out.

Zee glanced at Kostos.

"I think, considering the circumstances, we can allow Kostos access to this information," James said.

"Yeah," Nathan said. "I'm psychic."

Kostos looked between them. "There are no psychics in our reality."

"That's the party line, and we're going to keep it that way," Zee said, jiggling her box full of papers.

"This isn't looking good, y'all," Nathan said.

"Conspiracies never do," Kostos said. "James, do you mind if I pull my girlfriend into this? She… if anyone can be trusted, it's her. And considering her and my signatures were the first to come up on the computer's search, I'm worried."

"They may have you in their sights," James said. "If you tell me her location, I can bring her here in such a way that she will not be able to find this reality later. I do apologize, however, I-"

"Can't take any chances," Kostos said, holding up a hand. "Trust me, I get it. We live in San Diego."

Zee's stomach lurched as Kostos gave James their address.

They were living together?

"This will only take a moment," James said, disappearing.

"Kostos, can you set this all up in the dining room?" Nathan asked. "We'll get some coffee and food going. I have a feeling it's going to be a long night."

"Sure," he said, walking through the archway into James's fancy ass dining room and Zee followed, putting her box down on the table before following Nathan through double doors into the kitchen.

It was big and looked like a showroom kitchen as opposed to something actually used, like most of James's house, kept as impeccable and neat as him.

"Anal little shit, isn't he?" Zee said as Nathan got out the coffee beans.

"Zee," Nathan said.

"*Stop* right there," she said. "You've got your therapist tone on. I don't know where you're going, but *drop it*. We've got way bigger issues tonight."

"I…" He pressed his lips together. "You have a point. After this."

"Sure, let's pretend I'm actually going to go all girly and talk about my ex. That works."

"You have to deal with it eventually."

"Says who?"

He shot her a look and she winked, blowing him a kiss.

The slight crackle of the reality opening made Zee turn just as James walked through, a frozen and bound woman floating in behind him.

James snapped his fingers and the bindings released Rachel an inch above the floor.

She tapped down and brought her hands up so fast Zee didn't have time to react before she shot shards of solid water at him.

He smacked them down with a bored look.

"Rachel!" came from the doorway and she turned.

"Kostos?" she asked.

"It's okay. They're friends," he said, crossing the floor and pulling her into a bear hug. "I asked James to grab you. You… *we* might be in danger."

"But he's…" she pulled back and pointed between James and Zee. "And Zee's… Isn't James the bad guy?"

James laughed but there was no mirth in it.

"Propaganda, honey," Zee said. "Your bosses are looking like the bad guys. Well, and the Kings. Even if they aren't the ones killing people, they're still bringing deadly drugs in…"

She slammed her mouth shut.

No. Fucking. Way.

"Kostos!" She ran into the dining room and the group followed. "The autopsy reports on those chaos candy overdoses… you remember what any of them said?"

"I remember what all of them said," he said as she started picking through the folders. "Why?"

"What did they say? In general, I mean. How did they determine it was a drug overdose?"

"They all said chaos candy was found in the system."

"But we also have science reports saying they can't nail down exactly what chaos candy is or how it does what it does? How is that, if they have all these samples from people? At the very least they know the ingredients, to be able to tell that's what is in these people's systems, right?"

"Yeah, so they're faked, I thought we already knew that."

"Oh my god," Nathan said.

Zee finally looked up.

Kostos and Rachel looked confused, but Nathan's eyes were huge, his face frozen in shock.

And James's was stone solid.

He nodded once.

They both got it.

"Tell me I'm wrong, James," Zee said. "You have more experience with the Agency than all of us combined. Tell me this is *insane* and I'm in tinfoil hat territory. I mean, covering up some deaths by framing others is one thing, but…"

James shook his head. "I fear you are correct, Sarah. We have all been hoodwinked. It fits what we have found."

"What?" Rachel practically whispered, holding Kostos's hand so tight Zee could see her muscles straining.

"There is no chaos candy," Zee said. "No Kings. It was all made up by Agency, to give them a good cover for getting rid of people they didn't want around… and controlling the rest of us along the way."

"That's…" Kostos shook his head. "Impossible."

"You'd think."

Zee's head snapped around.

Jolnavich stood in a rip in front of the wall. "Really not that hard once you have control of the media. Thanks for going back to grab Rachel and leading us here. We've been trying to find and capture Dr. Morganson and his little protégé for years."

The rip expanded, showing a crowd of at least a dozen witches, power crackling and potions up.

Lindsey and Jarred right up at the front, grinning wide and proud of themselves, spells on and at the ready.

## CHAPTER EIGHT

Tricked.

This whole thing had been a set up. Maybe James was getting too close to something, or maybe the Agency just realized their whole coverup with the drugs thing would help them finally get the vampire who'd been a constant thorn in their side, but either way.

They'd played Zee like a pawn from the beginning.

"You have one chance to come quietly, Dr. Morganson," Jolnavich said.

"I believe the poor lackeys you sent after me earlier learned a most difficult lesson, that *that* is not a likely outcome," James said.

"Yes, well, we would have had you if Agent Darin had not disobeyed orders and stayed in that reality to find Zee when he was supposed to return to base to report."

Zee fought not to look over at Kostos.

He'd disobeyed orders to look for her?

"You and that psychic you're harboring don't come with us, these three die." Jolnavich jerked his chin towards the mortal witches.

Zee's heart seized.

They knew about Nathan.

"And we all know how you feel about protecting women," Jolnavich finished.

"I do feel very strongly about protecting women," James said. "That will not stop me from killing ones attempting to harm

143

innocent women or me. If you wish to take me alive"—James spread his arms wide—"you are quite welcome to try."

"George?" Rachel asked in a small voice. "We're *friends*. We've been to your house. I've babysat your kids. What are you doing?"

"Sorry, Rach." Jolnavich shrugged. "You two are good scapegoats for this whole debacle."

That's why her and Kostos's signatures were at the top of the list. They'd been recently brought up for this frame job.

Zee shook as she pulled her powers up.

Jolnavich and his entire goon squad practically glowed with power. Everything from natural abilities to premade spells and potions.

Five against at least a dozen.

And they were already tired.

"James?" Zee whispered.

"This is quite literally my world," James said. "If this man wants me, he will have to come in after me."

Jolnavich smiled.

Witches burst forward through the rip too fast to count, far more than the dozen Zee had seen.

They smacked against a shield she didn't even see get raised and James raised his hands.

About a third of the witches froze in place, James's natural ability to freeze things capturing only the weakest of the witches.

Zee and Kostos didn't waste any time, both bringing their powers up and zapping the frozen witches before they could shake it off, Zee with fire and Kostos with his lightning.

The floor rose on its own, swallowing one of the enemy.

The man barely had time to scream before the wood snapped back together, cutting him in half.

Nathan had backed into the corner and Zee could barely see him as he whispered off to the side.

Thousands of itty bitty bugs spilled out of the floor in front of Nathan, crawling for the intruders.

Two of the witches paled and ran back through the rip and Zee grinned.

It was never a good idea to go up against a psychic.

They could see your phobias and use them against you.

She took a deep breath and shot a wave of fire at Lindsey.

That bitch played on Zee's personal history of tragedy to get her on the case.

She was going down.

Lindsey blocked it and Zee pulled out her gun, shooting at Lindsey dead center, grateful for the spell to suppress the noise as it kicked in her hand.

The bullet smacked into a shield and dropped to the ground.

The others were in skirmishes all around the kitchen, James spelling so fast Zee's eyes couldn't track it, Kostos and Rachel fighting back to back, and Nathan conjuring fears so fast from the corner no one was able to get close to him without facing their deepest darkest terrors.

Zee grinned and faced down Lindsey.

"You're never going to win," Lindsey said, looking for all the world like a fanatic with the maniacal gleam in her eye.

"What happened to you?" Zee asked.

"We're doing what we have to to protect the people."

"No, you're doing what you have to to control them." Zee sent a blast at the bitch, heating the air around her to beyond what a human could withstand, making her sweat even through the shield, making the magic melt as it hit its tolerance.

Zee aimed and shot, the bullet getting stuck again, but falling on the other side of the shield.

Lindsey grunted and grinned over Zee's shoulder.

Zee dropped to her knees, shooting at Lindsey and turning so fast she didn't see if she actually got the woman as she shot up at whoever had been behind her.

The bullet bounced off Jarred's shield and up into the ceiling.

He backhanded Zee too fast for her to block.

Her face exploded and she cried out as she fell backward, gun skidding across the floor.

Jarred grabbed her arm and the world blinked away as they teleported into the room on the other side of the rip.

He slapped magic binding cuffs on her and grabbed her by her neck.

"Morganson!" Jarred yelled. "Surrender or she gets gutted."

Jarred produced a knife out of thin air and held it to Zee's neck.

She froze.

The room wasn't anywhere near the chaos it had been, most of the attackers dead, at least one curled up in a ball in the corner from whatever Nathan had showed her, a few left backing away as Zee's compatriots stopped to listen to Jarred.

James stared through the rip and looked from her captor to Zee.

She stared back and blinked once.

James nodded. "I surrender. Release her."

Jolnovich pulled a pair of handcuffs out and tossed them to James.

It was no surprise he'd managed to keep himself out of the fray.

The fucking coward.

"I put these on, you release Sarah, and let them all leave peacefully," James said, picking up the handcuffs.

"Not the psychic," Jolnovich said. "We need him."

Nathan didn't react.

James met Zee's eyes again and she blinked once.

James sighed. "Then it will be a trade of me for Sarah, and you may deal with Nathan on your own." He put the handcuffs on, face twisted up like he was smelling something nasty or wiping dog crap off his shoe.

Jarred snorted and let Zee go, running forward so fast he nearly tripped as he entered the next reality.

Zee pulled the small set of lockpicks off her belt and went to work on the handcuffs, getting out almost as fast as it took for Jarred to get to James.

She'd been getting out of handcuffs since she was first arrested at fifteen.

Her powers rushed back and she shot Jarred in the back with a concentrated bullet of superhot fire.

He screamed as he went up in flames.

Jolnovich turned as Zee launched herself back through the hole and flicked her away with a toss of his hand.

She flew through the air, slamming into Nathan and he grunted as they slammed into the pantry door.

"Ouch," Nathan said, standing in the superfluid vampire way.

He grabbed Zee's hand and pulled her up.

She was beyond feeling much of anything at this point.

The remaining witches stared at them, breathing deep and looking pretty wore.

Jolnovich however…

Zee's sight blazed when she looked at him.

He had some serious juice.

"James," she said.

"How much?" he asked, slinking around Jolnovich, already out of his handcuffs too.

"More."

She knew he'd understand the shorthand to mean more power than him.

Kostos rubbed his hands together, lightning crackling over his knuckles. "Run, cannon fodder. You're on the wrong side."

"No," James said. "They know how to enter my reality now. Until I can move it, they either must be killed or captured."

"Fine by me," Zee said, grabbing her gun. She walked over to James, Nathan close behind.

"You are welcome to try," Jolnovich said the same words James had mocked him with.

Secure in his power.

But he'd been fine sitting back and letting the others take the punishment, take the death, when he could've saved many of them just by joining the fight.

Kostos was right. Those poor warped fools were cannon fodder.

"He let you all fight while he stood on the sidelines," Zee said. "And he's got enough power to take on at least two of us by himself. But he kept his power and sent you all to fight. You really sure you're on the right side?"

The remaining three witches looked at each other, doubt making them so so young.

Jolnovich snorted, lifting a finger.

The three on the fence went up in flames.

Rachel screamed and Zee's shock was the only thing keeping her from doing the same.

"Can't trust foot soldiers who start thinking too much," Jolnovich said. "You know I had the perfect set up. Now I have to build my ranks again. Oh well, bunch of newbies will be coming to University soon."

"You will not live long enough to see it," James said.

"You're all exhausted," Jolnovich said. "I'm taking you in, Morganson. You and that poor simpleton you yanked away from me ten years ago."

"Don't let the accent fool ya," Nathan said, laying on the drawl. "Just 'cause we talk slow don't mean we are slow. And it's about time for you to learn that, you arrogant, yankie dick."

Nathan's eyes clouded and Jolnovich snapped a shield up.

But you never underestimate a psychic.

The dead bodies littering the floor pushed up, half torsos skootching across the floor, burned corpses standing on half cooked legs, all heading for Jolnovich.

He screamed, shooting magic out.

James pulled a gun out of the air, teleporting it from somewhere in the house, and walked up to Jolnovich, ripping through his shield with practiced precision while Jolnovich was weakened by his fear, and shooting the man from behind too fast for anyone to react, splattering the shield in the front with brains and blood.

The zombies dropped as Jolnovich fell.

Rachel turned and ran around the kitchen counter, barely hitting the pantry in time to throw up in the trash.

Kostos ran up to her, holding her hair and stroking her back.

"Right behind ya," Zee said, falling to her knees in the ichor.

"You know it goes higher than just Jolnovich," Zee said a few days later, sitting next to James in his kitchen.

"You believe it does," James said. "We do not have proof."

"The presidential candidate that turned up dead by seemingly unrelated causes but is somehow linked to all this says so," she said.

"That is a good point. However, after they destroyed the servers in San Diego, we do not have proof to take to anyone."

While they'd been fighting, one of the agents had slipped behind them and destroyed what they'd taken from the servers. And the next day, the servers in San Diego fell victim to an accident.

"Did Nathan find anything?" Zee asked.

"He is still looking. However, he can not risk stepping foot into the main reality or Parata, not now that the Agency knows of him and has samples of his magic to use to track him."

After the battle, Nathan went through the inn to hide in a new reality, essentially going into witches' protection, and Kostos and Rachel had debated following suit but they'd already decided they wouldn't. They'd go back to their jobs like nothing had changed, trying to find the rest of the corruption from within.

She sighed. "James... I don't think any of us should go back in there. Jolnavich said they had the media. That's not just a power-hungry cabal gone rogue in the government. That's a whole fucking conspiracy. That's Soviet Russia type control. And since this happened, it's not in the witches' news. It's all just there was an accident at the Agency headquarters in San Diego and at least two dozen agents were killed. That's… How do we fight that?"

"Day by day. Witch by witch," he said. "We make them see the propaganda for what it is. We encourage them to find the information for themselves, to set up their own structures. We keep building around, until we can fix what is within."

"Do you really believe Parata's government can be saved, James? That corruption and power that embedded, infection that deep, can be drained?"

"I do. It is merely a matter of educating new witches, one by one, so they know not to believe all they are taught in the school, teaching them to think for themselves, and then leaving them to grow and run for these offices, and one day dismantle this corrupted bureaucracy."

"I don't see it happening without a buttload of explosives, bulldozers and some bleach."

"Ah, but I am far older than you. I have seen the world, even the magical one, recover from far worse. Propaganda only holds hearts and minds until the paper it is written on starts to rip from the rewrites. Have hope, my dear. The fact that we can now see the corruption means it is crumbling."

"Hey, ol' blue eyes." Nathan appeared out of nowhere, making Zee hop in place. "New order forming."

"Ah," James said. "See, new witches to reach before the Agency does. This is how we do this. Where, Nathan?"

"Zee's birthplace. Salt Lake City, Utah. And these feel like powerful ones."

"Thank you. Have faith, Sarah. We have a psychic on our side."

James disappeared and Nathan grinned. "We got more than that." He tossed Zee a wink. "We got that fickle lady called fate playing for our team right now."

"What? Why?" she asked. "What did you see?"

"Let's just say I saw an itty bitty turning point in that vision I had. And she's a spitfire. Ol' blue eyes is about to meet his match. I can't see much beyond that, too many possibilities, but that order just may help us win this war. James is right. No matter how much control the government has, there's always hope. We just got to keep building."

Flux

-a teddy dormer story by-

Michael David Anderson

My name is Teddy Dormer, and up until recently, I was afflicted with a condition which inflicted insomnia upon others in my vicinity, consequently allowing me to experience their darkest dreams. I possessed no control over this ability and was subjected to it every night of my life. Now, however, I may experience others' dreams, but I no longer render them sleepless. The catalyst for these changes may be a concussion, but it may also be exposure to other individuals with odd abilities, each of them experimented upon and created by a shadow organization known in some circles as Black 9.

My life is now in a state of flux, for I am becoming something else. Don't misunderstand me: I'm still very much human, but my one defining condition has now been altered and I appear to be developing new abilities. Whereas before, I led a life of solitude and anonymity, Jessica Snow, my lover and long-time friend, now accompanies me on my journeys, for we both have been forced into exile in an effort to evade Black 9.

The following is an account of my experiences. It is neither fantasy nor fiction, despite what people would classify it as should they happen upon it. If this work ever does find its way onto bookshelves, it will be slapped with a FICTION label and sold as cheap entertainment by an author named Sullivan Doyle rather than under my own name for reasons I assure you would make no sense to most people. I do not write this memoir as a means of obtaining fame and fortune, but rather to chronicle the madness of leading such a life and to make sense of it. Call it therapy, if you will.

Should you come into possession of this memoir in its

intended form rather than publicized, this undoubtedly means I am certainly dead. If I were you, I would keep this a secret.

ONE

The night passed in a blur of shadow and headlights. Few vehicles populated the lonely road, and the trees disappeared into obscurity, illuminated only briefly ahead and then behind in an occasional red tinge of taillights.

I was tired, but only from the long drive. I was used to being lulled to sleep by the presence of others, but their somnambular habits no longer affected my consciousness. I was no longer a slave to their dreams and glad of it, but to feel so exhausted and be able to actively choose when I slept remained a foreign concept to me.

I glanced over at Jessica. She was reading a book I refused to read, but I knew its contents without having to ever read it. The author's name was not mine, yet I had written every word contained therein in a prior memoir.

With a mini-lamp clamped to the novel's rear cover, she read without assistance from the car's interior dome light. Jessica would look up occasionally and fix me with a peculiar look before asking a question regarding the story, and I would answer it without hesitation, although in response to a couple of questions regarding my feelings for her I would fumble. I am not used to romance, and to talk so openly about my feelings, especially with her, was an awkward exercise for me; to have my feelings laid bare in a book and then have to explain them further was downright humiliating, but I endured it.

Shortly after having left her hometown of Scarborough Hill, we learned of the existence of the book, which was named after me. I vowed never to crack its spine or to leaf through its pages; Jessica, however, was determined to devour its secrets, for she was convinced there may be a nugget of information contained therein that might prove crucial to our life moving forward. "Sullivan might have hidden a message for us in the story somewhere," Jessica explained the day she acquired her copy from a Ma and Pa bookstore. "If there's anything that will afford us an advantage, we need to know."

I didn't argue. When Jessica set her mind to something, she intended to proceed. I would not stop her, nor did I want to. She may be able to make better sense of my past than I could.

She tore her attention from the pages to fix me with her cool gaze. "This Noah guy was an asshole."

I didn't divert my gaze from the road. We were in the wilderness, and I knew one distracted glance away would be all it took for a deer to leap into the dual cones of brilliance illuminating the night and wreck our vehicle. I merely nodded, adjusting my grip on the steering wheel. "He was."

"And I can already tell Jill was a two-faced bitch," she added. "She's too damn *happy.*"

I already knew where she was in the story, and if you've read Doyle's novel, you may also know. "We're leaving the hospital, aren't we?"

"Yes, you are."

"I never should have gotten in their vehicle."

"But you did."

157

"And I shouldn't have."

"You're too hard on yourself," Jessica admonished, and returned her attention to the book.

Although I didn't look at her before, I dared a glance now, risking a suicidal deer to observe Jessica reading, a look of utmost peace and concentration upon her features. Of all the horrors we have been through both apart and together, it still amazes to me we should wind up here, together, and that I should be so lucky to be with someone not only breathtakingly beautiful but also a wonderful companion in every sense.

I returned my gaze to the road. We passed a speed limit sign indicating we should go no faster than eighty kilometers per hour. We had crossed the border into Ontario two days prior, and it was still odd adhering to the metric system rather than imperial. We had used passports under assumed names, but not the ones we ultimately decided we would use to settle down; we were on the run, after all, and thought it best to take every precaution to shake any potential pursuers. My contact, Will, arranged multiple identities for us, and we utilized them appropriately. For this leg of our journey, we were Alan and Tanya Pangborn. The officer at the border crossing had perked up, smiling, and asked me, "Are you the Sheriff of Castle Rock?" I didn't get the reference. After we pulled away, Jessica told me Alan Pangborn was the name of a character in a few Stephen King novels.

The long drive was getting the better of me. I yawned.

Without tearing her eyes off the page, Jessica said, "Perhaps we should find a place to stay for the night."

"I haven't seen a hotel in hours."

"Well, keep your eyes open. In the meantime, I'll look one up." And yet she kept reading.

I shot her a sideways glance.

"After I finish this page," she added.

I smirked.

Thirty seconds later, Jessica flipped the page, inserted her page mark, which was an illustriously designed Tarot card featuring a hanged man, switched off the reading light, and set the book in the backseat. She then pulled her phone from the space between her thigh and the seat and opened the internet search function. She voice-searched for nearby hotels along the projected route and waited as results slowly populated. She grimaced. "I'm not getting the best signal out here."

A break in the trees to the left rendered Jessica's search moot. The clearing revealed a parking lot and, at its end, a small inn. The building's nexus, where the two wings ultimately connected, looked like an oversized Victorian house, and the rest of the building's exterior matched its style. A sign out by the road featured a basic yet straight-to-the-point name – THE INN – and its Vacancy sign was illuminated in red neon.

"I think we found a place without the wonders of technology," I said.

Jessica frowned. "Of course, you did. You always do. I expect nothing less from a man who doesn't own a cell phone."

"They break too easily."

"Not if you handle them with care."

I laughed. "Are you actually *reading* that book? You know why I don't carry a cell."

Jessica rolled her eyes as I pulled into the parking lot. "Whatever you say, *Alan.*" She turned back to her phone. The results had finally populated, and she frowned. "That's weird."

"What's that?" I asked as I killed the engine.

"This place isn't on the map."

"That doesn't surprise me." I turned to her and winked. "A lot of places aren't on the map."

She smiled. "You would know."

"You have no idea."

I pulled the hatch release and got out of the car. We had traded Jessica's Toyota Tacoma for something better on gas mileage. It wasn't exactly my style – I preferred old school American muscle cars, having previously driven a Gran Torino and a Camaro in the past few months – but the Prius was spacious and accommodated our need to keep on the road for greater spans of time.

"I'll grab the bags," I told her as she stepped out into the night. The parking lot was mostly dark; there weren't many lights out here, but the few that were in evidence cast an oppressive gloom over the inn. The night was overcast, so moonlight wasn't available to further drive back the darkness.

"I'll help."

We rounded the back of the car, grabbed our essentials, and approached the front of the Inn. As we neared the front doors, the flesh on the back of my neck prickled and I shivered.

"You okay?" Jessica asked.

I nodded slowly, halting in my tracks. "I think so. Just a chill."

Jessica balled her fist and tapped my bicep. "Come on. The sooner we get checked in, the sooner we can both get some sleep."

"Yeah."

She led us inside, neither of us knowing then a majority of our night would not be spent sleeping.

TWO

The lobby of the Inn was spacious – and far larger than it had any right to be. The exterior of the building looked as though it could only contain a lobby approximately an eighth this size. Something about this place felt incredibly *off,* and my intuition told me to trust nothing I saw here.

The lobby itself was immaculate, with intricately designed, lavish chandeliers hanging overhead and amazing detail in the woodwork. I felt as if I had been transported to a wondrous hall built hundreds of years prior; the design felt simultaneously European yet... *alien,* as if this space were only meant to give an impression of one's expectations rather than accurately resemble one particular style.

Jessica and I had inadvertently stepped into the world of the weird once more. I was sure of it. Don't ask me how, but it was almost as if aspects of the Inn were manifesting before my eyes just before my gaze fell upon them, from the chandeliers overhead to the ornate carvings in the wood at the front desk, then losing focus as soon as I turned away. The effect was jarring. I rubbed my eyes and shook my head mid-stride.

Jessica led the way to the desk, where an ageless woman stood. She seemed both incredibly young and exceptionally old, both naïve and wise. I might have pegged her in her late twenties or early thirties, but something about her demeanor suggested she could have easily been twice that age despite the fact she could have easily tricked the producers of a film to think she was younger than my initial estimates. Her hair was a brilliant shade of auburn red, and her green eyes, which seemed to spark with tinges of hazel, pierced me with a single glance. She smiled at our approach. A name tag with her moniker – CINDYLOU – was pinned to the voluptuous curvature of her yellow blouse.

Hanging behind her, almost above her head, was an elaborate dreamcatcher: blue, and laced through with feathers and beads.

Jessica smiled and leaned forward at the counter, where, to her immediate right, a sign-in ledger sat. Accompanying the ledger wasn't a pen but a feather quill, and next to the ledger was a small ink container. A long list of signatures appeared on the sheet, some in messy scrawls, others in penmanship as fanciful as calligraphy.

I was used to talking to the house staff in hotels from years of driving from town to town, but since Jessica and I began traveling together, she had appropriated this duty. It wasn't something we discussed; she had simply become the architect of our stories whenever it was necessary, and I filled in details when prompted. In film, you often witnessed characters blunder through cover stories, but we complimented each other so seamlessly we might have been spies in another life.

Even as Jessica rested her forearms against the wood and leaned toward CindyLou, the vixen leaned forward as well and beamed, "Welcome to the Inn! I'm glad you can stay the night with us." Her voice, while even, contained a hint of southern twang to it, as if she had grown up in the south then spent years elsewhere, determined to rid herself of the accent.

Jessica laughed. "Out here in the middle of nowhere, I'm sure you don't get too many visitors."

CindyLou's smile widened, and I caught a glimpse of a fleeting, *knowing* look. "Oh, you'd be surprised. We get guests from everywhere."

I turned and surveyed the lobby. Save for the three of us, it was currently empty, or so I initially thought. Upon further investigation, I noticed a small game area at the far end of the chamber. Sitting in the corner on either side of a chess board were two gentlemen, one bare-chested, muscular yet toned, and scarred, the other dressed in a three-piece suit. As I watched them, the bare-chested gentleman drank from a mug of ale and set it back down with a sigh of satisfaction. He noticed me watching, offered a smug grin, and returned to his game.

I'm dreaming, I thought. *I have to be. This feels too much like a dream to be real.* My perception of reality coming into focus only as needed reinforced this idea.

"How much for a room?" Jessica asked.

"Thirty ought to do it."

Jessica raised an eyebrow. "Thirty even?"

"If you want to include gratuity, I won't mind."

Jessica shot me a quizzical look as she reached into her bag and extracted her own small wallet. From it, she retrieved thirty dollars in Canadian currency and handed them over.

"No gratuity," CindyLou pouted. "Pity. Sign the ledger, if you please. *Both* of you. We like to keep a record of our guests here at the Inn, after all."

Jessica dipped the quill in the ink and carefully scratched her name into being. She blanched, and I registered wonder and alarm in her eyes. She handed the quill over, and I went to sign my cover name beneath hers. Halfway through, I glanced up at hers. She should have signed Tanya Pangborn, but instead her name was as it was given to her: *Jessica C. Snow.*

After signing as Alan, I set the quill aside and studied my handiwork. I was aghast to find I had also signed my real name, middle initial *X* included, although I had purposefully made the movements to sign my alias.

CindyLou smiled. "The ledger isn't easily fooled, Mr. Dormer," she said. "You need not worry about hiding your true identities in these halls. The Inn saw fit to bring both of you here, after all." She handed Jessica the room key. Whereas most hotels had transitioned to electronic key cards, this was an actual key, and its handle featured an ornate design. Jessica turned it end over end as she studied it. "You're in Room 2119. Enjoy your stay."

An uneasy seed of worry churned in my stomach. I shook my head and said, "I don't believe we'll be staying after all."

CindyLou's smile faded. "I don't believe you can leave just yet. You won't be able to drive away. I've noticed your car is no longer out the front doors."

Alarm seized both of us, and as we turned, Jessica demanded, "Did someone jack our car?"

I was already halfway across the lobby when CindyLou said, "No, it's exactly where you left it."

I didn't understand how the car could still be where we left it yet not outside. As I approached the doors, however, a part of me began to understand. The primal part, I'd say, because the reasonable part of my consciousness couldn't grasp what I was seeing: Although the parking lot was gloomy upon our arrival, it was now a pitch-black maelstrom of shadows.

"It is rare that someone should walk through the front doors as if this were an ordinary hotel," CindyLou said from behind the counter. Turning, I found she hadn't moved from her spot, and regarded us with a look of both concern and understanding. "Many of our guests arrive by other means, through doors unseen, from locations far and wide. Your arrival here must mean you are uniquely suited to address an issue here at the Inn. There may be one I either do not entirely understand or which has already manifested I am currently unaware of." CindyLou's eyes shifted to the right then: a telltale sign she was evading the truth.

I exchanged a glance with Jessica. The look in her eyes worried me, for her confusion and concern was evident. My concern, however, wasn't for the threat of danger, but for my role in whatever events may be developing. After our experiences in Scarborough Hill, my self-confidence had tanked. I no longer understood my place in the universe because my comprehension of the world around me had been irrevocably changed. Whereas before I plunged into danger blindly, determined to thwart the machinations of evil, I now questioned if my presence in such situations merely exacerbated them.

"I don't know who you think I am," I said, my tone measured yet shaky to my own ear, "but I assure you I am in no position to help you."

"But you are," CindyLou said. "You may question your resolve, but I see it in your eyes, both of you. If there is anything you need ask of me, please don't hesitate. However, for now, I highly suggest you retire to your room." She waved her arm to indicate the nearby staircase. "Something tells me you'll need your rest for whatever is to come."

## THREE

I led the way upstairs, noting as we went that the staircase and the halls beyond reminded me of the Overlook in *The Shining,* casting a surreal quality to our environs. I felt like I was dreaming, but I knew I was awake.

CindyLou had insisted we leave our belongings at the desk. "Don't you worry about them," she said. "Our bellhop will have them right up."

As we entered the wing in which our room awaited us, we found the bellhop already waiting for us, our small amount of luggage on the cart at his side. From a distance, he looked like a mummy with the wraps removed from his face. His aged façade was decrepit, almost as if it might disintegrate at the slightest provocation, and his tattered uniform, grimy and looking as if it had spent many years in the company of mothballs, looked like it belonged in a bygone era and had been stored long-term in a dusty closet. As we came closer, however, his countenance changed, as did his uniform, his overall appearance shifting from ghostly to lively. His face changed most of all, from that of a cadaver to a teenager with pimples and dimples. His hair was a shade south of copper, whereas before its color had been indiscernible. His name tag revealed his name was Ron.

He smiled, his head full of pearly teeth so white I was certain they were painted, and I was momentarily convinced the kid must be a ventriloquist dummy. Once I was within arm's length, he extended his own and, without waiting for me to actively participate, vigorously shook my hand with an exceedingly firm grip, jostling my arm so much I was afraid he might dislocate my shoulder. "It's nice to make your acquaintance, Mr. Dormer!" He let go of me, turning to Jessica, and immediately engaged in an equally violent handshake with Jessica. "You as well, Ms. Snow. Welcome to the Inn!"

"Thank you," Jessica said, retracting her hand. She was not one to openly invite physical contact with others in most circumstances, and I noted Ron's invasion of her personal bubble made her intensely uncomfortable. Her trust of others was shattered at a young age, and many individuals over the years had strengthened that sense of isolation she holds dear. I am an exception to the rule, for she trusts me implicitly, a fact of which I am both cautiously aware and eternally grateful. In the weeks prior to this night, I had been a ship lost at sea, but she was my rudder, my guide and constant companion.

"If you don't mind, Ron," she said, making a point to pause and read his name tag as she spoke, "we'd both like to retire for the evening. It's been an exhausting day, and our arrival here has only served to make us wearier. We're not used to slipping into pocket universes or whatever this place might be."

Ron smiled at that. "Yes, yes, I understand! But miss, this isn't a pocket universe. It's a nexus point in the space *between* worlds."

Her smile was strained, an attempt at kindness and civility, when she added, "That only solidifies my point."

Ron's smile faltered. "Yes, yes, I'm sure it does. My apologies, miss." I noticed his eyes flick past us, registering the arrival of another guest in the hall.

I turned and, with a shock of sudden but unsure familiarity, observed an older gentleman. He wore a custom-tailored tuxedo which gave him a paradoxical look, although he seemed aloof and stepped with the grace of a slow-motion ballerina; the tux itself was rigid on his body, its cut so sharp it might cut anyone with whom he dared come in physical contact. He shot us a glance from above his ridiculously bushy mustache, the tips of which were curled upward with an effect that made him look quite dastardly. His eyes were an alarming shade of scarlet, as if his irises were pools of blood, and his hair, short beneath his top hat, was a sleek black and as rigid as the rest of his suit, rendering his mustache far more ridiculous. Sticking out of the white band encircling his top hat was a Tarot card, which appeared to be a dancing skeleton.

Death.

As I alluded moments ago, the gentleman struck a chord of recognition, but from where I could not recall. I racked my brain for the answer, but it would not come willingly; it eluded me, dancing just beyond my powers of recollection, a memory monkey taunting me as it danced from foot to foot, arms flailing as it hooted at me.

He produced his own key, inserted it into the lock, and with a flourish of his coattails vanished into his room.

"He says his name is Bartholomew Barthandelus," Ron said, the former excitement in his voice now gone. He sounded cautious, afraid. "He's been with us a couple days now. His presence has perverted the Inn. There's even a brothel in the east wing that wasn't there before!"

The suggestion inherent in his statement intrigued me. "Wait. Are you telling me this place can change at will based on whoever is here at the time?"

Ron looked at me then, dumbfounded. "I'm sorry, I'm not used to visitors who do not understand the power of this place. Yes, the Inn changes. Sometimes the changes are small. At others, the manifestations are quite thorough. I'm *still* noticing differences since Mr. Barthandelus's arrival. Since your arrival, there have been a few, but not as widespread as his effects. To be frank, the man gives me the heebie jeebies." He shuddered, closed his eyes, and composed himself. "Here, let's get you into your room."

Ron didn't produce a key, opting instead to simply wave his hand over the doorknob, and the door opened with a click, swinging wide to afford us a view of the room beyond. The space was identical to a room I occupied at the Comet Tail Inn. It was burned into my memory due to a dream I experienced in which I encountered the Man of Shadows, an entity that tore through the walls, creating cracks from which lava had issued forth.

A chill tiptoed my spine.

"It's always interesting to see how the rooms manifest," Ron noted. "This room looks rather... bland."

He pushed the cart in, set our bags against the wall, and turned to leave. As he did, his attention was drawn to the far side of the room, beyond my field of vision at the threshold. "That certainly seems out of place here."

Frowning, I stepped into the room, Jessica following close behind. Above the bed was a painting, its frame an intricate array of golden curlicues. Set within it was a lavish painting set in a bleak, snowy landscape. The moon was full in one corner, and massive. A figure in a crimson cloak stood at the edge of a cliff, head turned, face hidden in the shadows beneath his hood. One arm was raised and brandished an absurdly large sword above his head, its blade gleaming brilliantly in the moonlight.

The painting had not been in my room at the Comet Tail.

"I'll leave you be," Ron said, slipping past us. "If you require anything of us, please don't hesitate to contact CindyLou at the front desk."

He pushed the cart out of the room, and the door closed seemingly of its own accord. Once he was gone, I sat on the bed and regarding Jessica with a look of urgency.

Jessica doesn't question me in situations such as this; in fact, she's usually on the page upon which I find myself just before I am, and while she may not know everything I've endured, she knows to trust my instincts. The only question she posed now was simple and direct: "What do we do?"

"I need you to put me under," I said.

"That much I assumed," she replied. "But why?"

"Barthandelus," I stated, tasting the name on my tongue. It felt inherently false. Not evil, perhaps, but merely window-dressing. I doubted the gentleman's true name was Bartholomew Barthandelus; it sounded not only pretentious but absurd as well. How he might have fooled the front desk ledger, however, was beyond me. "I've seen him somewhere before, but I don't know where."

Jessica stepped to a spot roughly three feet in front of me. As she knelt, she said, "You think he's why the Inn brought us here."

I nodded.

"How sure are you?"

I smirked. Rather than saying it simply, a phrase crossed my mind, and I couldn't pass up the opportunity to say it. "My conviction is strong."

"You dolt."

"You love me."

170

"And you love me." She folded her legs underneath her and sighed. "Are you ready for this?"

I shook my head. The events in Scarborough – and since – had rattled me. Now that we were here, however, there wasn't much that could be done to avoid our circumstances. I would rather do as I always had done and face trouble head-on rather than dally and wait for it to not only come for me but catch me unprepared. "Absolutely not," I told her. I closed my eyes and exhaled. "Let's do this."

"Yes," she said. "Let's."

FOUR

The weeks after Scarborough Hill burned were an endless nightmare for me. I was dealing with the side effects of a concussion, which for someone like me proved to be nothing short of disastrous. It deprived me of true sleep and submerged me in a sea of waking dreams. My memory of those two weeks is sporadic at best and more often than not a discombobulated mess. Freddy Krueger himself, if the dream master were in fact *real* rather than a movie creation, could not have devised a dreamscape such as the one in which I was lost.

I have asked Jessica about what she witnessed during that time. She refuses to tell me. Because of this, as she knelt before me to begin the process, I failed to mention I was convinced I had seen Bartholomew Barthandelus in the madness I experienced following our escape from Scarborough Hill. This willful excursion into my subconscious would be a horrific one, but if I

171

was to extract any knowledge regarding what I had seen about the gentleman down the hall, this was it.

I didn't know if we had already crossed paths with Barthandelus before arriving at the Inn. In the time since my insomniac mania, I have discovered my former nighttime habits have changed. Those around me no longer experience insomnia, nor am I subjected to dreams randomly. I may be drawn to the dreams of those around me, but I have a new level of control not only in selecting the dreams I may experience but also how I may interact with them. During the time when I was concussed, however, everything was chaotic, and to make sense of my experiences then was impossible.

Once the mania subsided, I found the first few days filled with a natural, restful sleep I had never known. As the days passed, however, I was cursed with an inability to fall asleep willfully and would often toss and turn. It was for this reason Jessica devised a method of leading me into the realm of the Sandman.

I closed my eyes and listened as she softly hummed a lullaby, occasionally clicking her tongue to disrupt the melody. The disruption prevented me from succumbing entirely to rest and kept my mind engaged even as I was lured into a restful state.

I imagined the room in which we performed the ritual. The walls, the painting, the bed, the television on the furniture stand. One by one, they faded from existence until all that remained was me, suspended in the void of my subconscious. Distantly, I could still hear Jessica, but she too was fading. Soon, I would be left alone with nothing but my thoughts.

I focused on my breathing: in, out, in, out, every exhalation a purpose, every inhalation a gift.

I recalled the room in which I had been treated after leaving Scarborough Hill. We rendezvoused with Will, and through one of his contacts I received medical attention for my many injuries. I had been fading from reality then, caught in a loop of nightmarish visions. Will brought me water at one point, and when I looked at his face, it was an abomination: eyes gone, a grotesquely large centipede extending out of his mouth and curling into one open eye socket and out the other, its mandibles twitching ferociously.

The image was burned into my mind, and although Will did not appear before me, dark spots bore through the walls, eradicating them and allowing countless centipedes to emerge, bodies twitching and arching madly as they emerged from the void. One by one, they dropped from the holes in the dreamscape, each one a minimum of six inches long, many well over a foot in length.

The centipedes were not my fear, but Will's. I knew they could not harm me. Therefore, I moved through the writhing masses on the floor, nonplussed.

We met Will at a hotel initially, but my treatment occurred at his house once we had taken steps to ensure we would not be pursued. I navigated his house of centipedes, unsure if I was recalling it in its entirety despite my mind's ability to fill in the blanks as I did so. The imagination is a powerful engine, creating and understanding almost simultaneously. This, like the endless dreamscapes into which I intruded throughout my life, was a marvel despite its creepy crawly proclivities.

This was not truly Will's house. It was merely a surrogate for the mysteries awaiting me within my own memory. It was here I had begun the true descent into madness. It seemed only fitting as far as I was concerned to begin my exploration here.

I followed a long hallway, passing through an increasingly labyrinthine structure of rooms. I witnessed a plethora of horrors I both recognized and unfamiliar to me, serving as echoes of psyches I had encountered throughout the years but hadn't fully explored. The countless individuals my mind had touched throughout my life left an imprint in its deepest recesses, creating a nightmarish cabinet of curiosities. These echoes could arise despite my lack of memory regarding them.

Some of these horrors were typical - psychotic clowns, rabid dogs, faceless men and women, a legion of cockroaches – but some proved to be far more personal and unsettling, like the reanimated corpses of beloved, mangled children. I passed each of these rooms without hesitation or fear, for I have been exposed to horrors regularly and have been desensitized to mere nightmares.

In one room, the Man of Shadows lingered. The dark figure stood in a brightened room, his eyes ablaze with hellfire, his mouth a grinning rictus of flame. "You seek the unexplained," he said, his voice the rasp of a thousand discordant demons. Somewhere in the dissonance of his voice, I could hear the distinct cadence of Noah Parkman's voice masked by the distortions of others. "Barthandelus usurps the unknown."

"Enough with your unintelligible babble," I told him, waving a flippant hand at him. The cynosure of shades erupted into a paroxysm of flame and smoky darkness only to dissipate into the ether.

Had the Man of Shadows truly been an entity separate from my own subconscious, I would have taken his words as a validation of my suspicions regarding Barthandelus. However, I surmised he was merely acting as a conduit for my own thoughts.

I rounded a corner only to find myself face to face with an

abrupt end to the corridor, and in that cessation stood a solitary hotel door. A DO NOT DISTURB sign featuring a dancing skeleton in a top hat hung from the knob. I ignored the sign and disturbed the sanctity of the room beyond, although I didn't dare knock; instead, I turned the door knob, which wasn't locked, as I doubted it would be. After all, I'd been here before, weeks earlier.

I strode into the dark room within to find a young boy. His flesh emanated an unsettling crimson glow, but his scarlet eyes called my attention. I didn't know if it was the aura about him, but I realized I could not determine his age or the size of his body; his physical stature seemed to be in a constant state of flux. At one moment, he seemed smaller, as if he were no more than five or six years old, and at others as large and mature as a teenager on the cusp of adulthood. Another glimpse, and he seemed ancient before a blink reset his apparent youth. His ears, I noticed, were elongated like an elf's... if elves existed, that is.

"Help me," he said, his voice another amalgamation similar yet purer than that emanating from the Man of Shadows. Here, I was certain the voice remained the same despite the changes and that I was hearing it at every age rather than from a single time period. "Help Opopanax."

I frowned. "Opopanax?" I asked.

The shifting face nodded. "Opopanax," he confirmed. "Barthandelus is *feeding.*"

## FIVE

I rose through the foggy layers of consciousness, and when I opened my eyes and regarded Jessica, she knew I'd found something. "What?" she asked.

"I'm not entirely sure," I replied, frowning. "Have you ever heard of Opopanax?"

"Opopanax?" she repeated, tasting the world in her mouth. "No. I can't say I have."

I explained about the ageless boy in the hotel room, repeating his words to Jessica: *Help me. Help Opopanax. Barthandelus is* feeding.

"Feeding? You don't think he's a cannibal, do you?"

I shook my head. "No, something tells me this is stranger and less straightforward than cannibalism."

"Either way," she said, rising to her feet, "we need to get into his room."

"Yes, but we don't know what we're up against here. After what happened in Scarborough, I'm reluctant to go in, blind."

"We could call CindyLou."

"She said to call if we needed anything."

"Exactly."

I nodded.

Jessica went to the phone. She started to check the underside of the handle to see if there were any instructions, but even from across the room I could hear the line ringing, and she put the phone to her ear. The line connected, and through it I heard a man's voice, loud and clear even from across the room. "Front desk."

"Yes, is CindyLou available? This is Jessica Snow in 2119."

"Ah yes, Miss Snow. I'm afraid CindyLou has stepped away. She has other urgent matters to which she must attend. I'm Sam. How might I be of assistance to you and Mr. Dormer?"

Jessica's eyes indicated she was at a loss, unsure of how to proceed. I twirled my finger in a *go on* gesture. She nodded. "CindyLou was under the impression we were brought here for a reason. We think we've determined one of the Inn's current guests may have kidnapped someone and is currently holding them in his room."

A measured moment of silence from the other end of the line ensued. After great consideration, Sam spoke. "I see. This still doesn't answer the question of what I can do for you."

"Is there any way of knowing if Bartholomew Barthandelus has left his room or is still in it?"

At the front desk, Sam cursed. "I knew there was something about that man. I couldn't *see* what it was though. It was beyond my abilities. I believe he's still in his room. Do you need him drawn out?"

"Yes."

"Very well. I'll have a skeleton key brought to your room. I must impress upon you the singular uniqueness of this situation. You must not abuse this privilege."

"Believe me, we fully understand."

"Good." Sam sighed. "Give me some time. I have a feeling Sir Barthandelus is a formidable adversary. While there are other dangerous men and women in the Inn, I would rather avoid an

177

outright confrontation in these halls, especially when a man such as he – if he truly *is* a man – is an unknown factor in the equation."

I sensed Sam suspected something about Barthandelus, but I didn't know how to broach the subject, not with Jessica the one on the line, and she did not ask. Instead, she said, "Thank you, Sam."

"Don't mention it," he replied, and terminated the call.

SIX

Ten minutes later, a soft knock punctuated the silence. I darted to my feet and crossed the room. Outside, I found a pixie of a girl – lithe and elvish, ears elongated similarly to the boy's in the dream, her skin flawless, its tone seeming to darken and fade in accentuated flourishes only a paint brush should be able to create. Her body was unmarked by tan lines, and her skin didn't seem to abide by the standard rules of pigmentation, for she was fair skinned in some regions and cocoa in others. I was able to determine this primarily due to her state of dress, or lack thereof; she wore lacy white and blue undergarments which left only the most private portions of her body to the imagination. Her hair, which alternated through a variety of pink and purple hues, was pinned up by a golden scarab pin.

The girl regarded me with a raised eyebrow. "Dormer?"

I swallowed, realizing with an uncomfortable twinge of guilt I had been unabashedly studying her body. "Yes."

She reached into the crevice between her breasts and

withdrew a key, its ornate handle featuring a grinning skeleton amongst interwoven strands of gold. "Give me a couple minutes to draw him back to the brothel."

I took the key from her. "Be careful."

She smirked. "Oh, don't you worry about me, honey. If he's nothing less than a gentleman, I'll make sure *everyone* knows he ain't a gentleman for the rest of his days." She flashed her pearly whites and chomped them together for dramatic effect.

Behind me, Jessica laid a hand on my shoulder and peeked past me. "Thank you for doing this."

She smiled. "No, thank you. Anyone who brings trouble to this Inn needs to be sorted out. We all appreciate you coming here."

I thought again about Ron's comment regarding the brothel and how it had not been a fixture in the Inn before Barthandelus's arrival. "You work in the brothel?"

She smiled. "Yes."

"Forgive me, but how are you a regular here? Ron gave us the impression the brothel isn't normally open."

The girl's smile widened. "How, indeed," she said, then turned and began to walk down the hall, her footfalls the merest whispers of echoes.

"Wait," Jessica said, halting the girl's progress. She turned toward us, her gaze inquisitive. "Let me slip ahead. I'll give Teddy the all clear once you're downstairs."

The girl nodded. "Good thinking."

Jessica slipped past me. As she joined the working girl in the hall, she showed me the walkie in her hand. "Yours is on the bed." I nodded. She turned, whispering something to the girl just beyond my earshot, then continued on down the hall, and disappeared down the stairwell.

The girl waited outside Barthandelus's door. I gave her a curt nod before slipping back into my room. Once the door was closed, I retrieved my walkie, turned it on, and depressed the trigger. "Mic check, mic check."

Jessica's voice burst through a crackle of static like a firework. "I read you loud and clear, darling. I'll let you know when you're good to go."

"Thanks."

There was a pause before she spoke again. "What do you think you're going to find in there?"

I considered what I had seen in the dreamscape, how the figure had been simultaneously young and old, shifting between the two as if time and age were both amorphous concepts.

I told Jessica the truth. "I have no idea."

I sat on the edge of the bed.

"By the way, I saw you checking out that girl."

I scoffed. "I don't know what you're talking about."

"Oh, yes you do! It was kind of hard *not* to check her out. Hell, *I* was checking her out, and I'm not into chicks."

I shook my head, pressing the walkie against my forehead. I said nothing.

"She wasn't leaving much to the imagination, which is in our favor if she's going to get Barthandelus out of his room and back to the brothel."

"Let's hope so."

Then there was silence. I pondered what the boy meant when

180

he said *Help Opopanax;* my ability to help was severely hindered by my lack of knowledge. I hoped answers awaited me inside Barthandelus's room.

The walkie barked to life once more. "You're clear. Go."

"Copy."

I rose, ready to move, but I realized that, if I were to encounter any danger in the minutes and hours ahead, I may not be able to adequately defend myself as I was. In the past, I have always been resourceful in extricating myself from predicaments, but with time I have found myself in far tighter jams. My time in Scarborough Hill only solidified this point for me, for I had been forced to act with deadly force.

I have never liked firearms. Whereas I believe people should be able to protect themselves, the idea of personally taking someone's life via projectile has always made me feel not only uncomfortable but tainted. Before the past year, I had never been forced to take another's life; now, I had taken several, the last of which had been by firearm.

Desmond. His sister, Izzy, died as well, although not because I shot her. I'm not entirely sure if I can count her as a direct casualty of my actions, but I *feel* like she was.

I wrestled with my need for a weapon, knowing it was sensible, but my sensibilities cried out against it. I have never fancied myself to be an action hero like Jack Bauer or Jason Bourne, characters who kick ass and take names as well as shoot first and ask questions later. Times change, however, and so must I, because the inability to change and evolve inevitably leads to death and extinction.

I went to my bag, pocketing the walkie as I went, and found my new weapon of choice, a Sig Sauer P227. Will had been sure to hook Jessica and I up with firepower before we parted ways. "It's a dangerous world out there," he'd said. "It's best you go into it prepared."

I checked the P227 to ensure it was loaded with the safety on, then tucked it into my back waistband and pulled my shirt down over it.

From bed to door, from door to hall, through the hall to Barthandelus's quarters, I went with single-minded purpose. As soon as I reached his door, I inserted the skeleton key, turned it, and heard the lock disengage. I opened the door and slipped into the dark room beyond. I flipped the light switch, but there was no power.

The room couldn't have been more different than the one in which Jessica and I were staying. This space wasn't simply a room but a log cabin, and every surface was encrusted with what could have easily been a millennia's worth of dust. Across the living area, floor to ceiling windows, partially obscured by age and grime, offered a panoramic view of a dark, snowy vista. The nearest trees were barren and black, and the cloudy night sky blocked out the moon and stars.

I lifted the walkie and depressed the trigger. "I'm in," I said, but when I let go of the trigger, I noted there was no telltale sign of the static indicative of a connection. I hesitated, then tried the walkie again. "Jessica, do you read?"

Nothing.

Observing the dark landscape beyond the windows, I realized the likelihood I was still in the Inn was slim to none. Somehow, the room to Barthandelus's quarters served as a portal to his true base of operations elsewhere. I'd left the Inn.

"Well, shit."

I pocketed the walkie. For now, I was on my own.

The cabin's living room was a mausoleum. Had it contained sarcophagi in the corners and in the center of the room, I would not have been entirely surprised, but there did not appear to be any sign of mummified remains in this part of the residence. However, while there were no sarcophagi, the treasures of those who would have been buried here remained, not as gold and artifacts and trinkets, but as books, magazines, vinyl records, and films, VHS and discs alike. They were piled high in stacks throughout the entirety of the residence, in many places waist-high, in others even higher, and I perused the titles as I went, for the night beyond, as starless and moonless as it was, surprisingly afforded enough light to see. I studied the treasures, brushing dust away so that I may observe them unimpeded.

To the left, I noted several films on disc and tape, all of which I knew, with my knowledge of pop culture, should not exist. One, a Marilyn Monroe film titled *Something's Got to Give,* was never completed, for the leading lady died in the midst of production and the film was abandoned. Nonetheless, the cover featured Monroe in a pool, smiling seductively, arms out of the water as she lifted herself up. Her shoulders were bare, and the slightest hint of the swell of her breasts rose above the side of the pool. The cover was an obvious allusion to what was intended to be the first true skinny-dipping scene by an A-list star in Hollywood; it would have been a hell of a draw for the studio had the film been completed.

Other films caught my eye, such as *Star Trek: Planet of the Titans, Phantasmagoria: The Visions of Lewis Carroll, Superman Lives!, Batman Triumphant,* a version of *Triumphant*'s predecessor *Batman & Robin* featuring Bruce Willis as Mr. Freeze, *and Spider-Man 4,* featuring a cover with the Tobey

Maguire Spidey and John Malkovich as the Vulture. Beyond them, I noted book titles that didn't exist as well, including Shakespeare titles *Jesus of Nazareth*, *Love's Labours Won*, and *Cardenio*, as well as several Stephen King novels: *Sword in the Darkness*, *The House on Value Street*, and *The Cannibals*.

Past the Stephen King titles was a stack of Sullivan Doyle novels, with *In the House of Wolves* and *Nyctophobia* among the first two. More awaited beneath them. I shuddered to consider how many there were.

I tore my eyes from the titles. This room was a treasure trove of things that weren't meant to be.

I checked the rooms to the right. There, I found countless stacks of items, the nearest of which included VHS copies of *Revenge of the Jedi* and *Back to the Future* featuring Eric Stoltz as Marty McFly. Other than the things that could not be, there was no sign of the boy, or man, or whatever.

I ventured past the sofa in the living room, knocking over a stack of old newspapers as I went. I didn't bother checking the headlines. I'd seen enough. If there were endless pop culture changes collected in this place, I didn't want to know what events had come to pass in elsewheres and whens. To go down that road was madness.

The kitchen was unoccupied. To its right, a ladder led up to a loft. I climbed it and discovered the space above was far tidier than the main floor; it lacked the hoarded stacks.

I was nearly ready to give up this fool's errand, to return to the Inn and re-establish contact with Jessica, when I noticed the small door in the corner. It was roughly two and a half feet tall, just large enough for me to crawl through, and featured a padlock, but it wasn't engaged. Anyone could get in, but no one or nothing behind the door could get out.

I went to the door, pulled the lock off, and pocketed it. I dared not leave it out here; if Barthandelus were to return, he could easily lock me in if he so chose; I would not become a prisoner so easily. I pushed the door inward, revealing naught but darkness, and climbed through a veil of musk that offended my olfactory glands. I gagged. Strands of cobweb hung about my face, but it appeared as if someone's previous passage had knocked away the wall which should have greeted me.

In the darkness, a voice rasped, "Hello?" I returned the greeting, and the owner of the voice choked a sob. "Oh, thank the gods. I was afraid it was him."

My eyes adjusted to the gloom, and I saw a figure tied with wire, hands behind his back. His face was drawn and gaunt, deeply lined with wrinkles, his blonde, shaggy hair obscuring half his face. Despite this, the half I could see appeared quite young, as if the wrinkles were a side effect not of age but something else. He wore a tunic and cloth pants, both of which were ragged and only hinted at the ravages of malnutrition underneath. His eyes were his most lively feature, for they blazed a fierce and unsettling red.

"What has he done to you?" I asked. "How long have you been here?"

"He's feeding upon my mana," he said, coughing. "I'm not sure how long I've been here. Time is... *funny* here."

Time isn't all that's funny here, I thought.

I scuttled past him, settling on my knees. "Let me get you out of this," I said, working on the wire binding his wrists.

As his bonds loosened, he sighed with relief. "Pray tell, what is your name?"

185

"Teddy."

"I am Vayne Opopanax, the thirty-seventh of my line."

The thirty-seventh of his line? I wondered. "I'm not sure I understand what you mean."

I finished untying his wrists, and he gasped, pulling his hands forward and rubbing the lacerations where the wire had cut into his flesh. "Opopanax found me," he explained. "I was chosen. Many have come before me, and unless I die here in this gods-forsaken cabin, many more will come after."

I helped him with the wire encircling his ankles. "Vayne, I'm sorry, but I have no idea what you mean."

"Opopanax is a spiritual life force," he said, grunting with effort as he pulled at a length of wire. "It is the source of my mana. Barthandelus feeds on mana, and therefore I can sustain him in ways others can't."

"Okay, that makes a lot more sense," I replied, shaking my head. "Freaking weird, but it still makes more sense."

We unwound the rest of the wire, and he stretched his legs, groaning as he did so. "We have to go before he gets back. I can't face him, not like this. I'm too weak to call on my mana."

The walkie in my pocket squawked, and Jessica's urgent voice cut through a burst of ear-splitting static: "*-you can hear this, get out. Get out NOW, Teddy. He's com-*"

Then silence.

I had lost contact with Jessica as soon as I entered the cabin and closed the door to the Inn. Therefore, I surmised Barthandelus must have opened his room door and entered the cabin. When he closed the door, he'd cut off my line of communication with her once more.

186

Vayne and I exchanged looks. Our time, it seemed, was running dreadfully short.

SEVEN

I was worried about being locked in the crawl space with Vayne, but I did not wish to be discovered here with nowhere to run. At least atop the loft, I might have better options for escape even if the only safe way down was the ladder.

I led Vayne out the way I entered and emerged, huddling, in the corner of the loft. He followed, grimacing as he rose to his feet. I shuddered to think how long he'd been tied up in that chamber. I'm not claustrophobic, but the very nature of that space, with its oppressive darkness and abundance of cobwebs, could induce an anxiety attack in anyone, myself included.

I didn't bother to close the door behind us. I pulled the Sig Sauer from my waistband and, rising to my full height, approached the ledge.

Below, the old gentleman in the top hat was awaiting my reveal, standing amidst the labyrinth of things that should not be as he studied the loft. He was not surprised. Instead, he merely lifted his hands and applauded me in melodramatic fashion. "That was a clever ploy, sending Pixie to call on me. I've never been one to deny the pleasures of the flesh."

"You should leave," I said. "I've already freed your prisoner, and I have the high ground. There's no outcome in which you come out of this situation on top."

Barthandelus smirked. "So you say. However, I detect the

slightest tremble in the hand which brandishes that pistol. You may have shot a man before, but you're not comfortable with the notion either. There's a high probability you'll miss your shot, and while you may have the high ground, do not believe for a second that means you have an advantage over me, young man. I've played this game for *centuries*. You are but a pup. It would be wise for you to surrender. You may still walk away from this with your life."

I, of course, had no intention of surrendering. His words, however, did arouse questions with answers I could not fathom. *Centuries?* I had encountered a man previously who had learned how to extend his life by possessing the bodies of others as he died. I had not decided if he was simply a ghost or demon; however, he was the only entity I had encountered who had survived for centuries. To be confronted by another with the same supposed lifespan, I wondered if he was another of his kind or something else.

"I sense your hesitation," Barthandelus continued. "No doubt you are considering my words. You do not seem the type to lay down your arms, but I will give you this opportunity. Will you surrender? Do we have an accord?"

Behind him, Jessica appeared from the short foyer through which I had passed earlier. The staff, I assumed, must have provided her with another key. She was armed and held our adversary in her gun sights.

I curtly shook my head. "No, we don't." I lifted my gun, aiming at him as well. I kept Jessica in my peripheral vision, making a point not to look directly at her lest I make her presence known.

Barthandelus sighed. "Such a shame."

The change which overcame him was instantaneous. He lifted his arms, and his face contorted in a scarlet effusion as he arched his neck and silently howled at the ceiling. I could not tell if the emission was simply light or partially fluid, but it emanated from his flesh much like the regeneration energy from the Time Lord in *Doctor Who* and bathed the entire cabin in its eerie glow. His head snapped down, his eyes enraptured with murderous glee, and he roared. *"You sniveling little shit! You won't stop me from completing the Ritual of Yuul! I will feed on Opopanax, and I'll eat your worthless soul for dessert!"*

A blast of scarlet erupted from his face and I dove aside, losing my grip on my Sig Sauer. The energy burst ripped through the loft, disintegrating wood, showering me with splinters. With dismay, I realized the top of the ladder had vanished, undoubtedly eradicated in the blast.

I turned, finding Vayne on the floor behind me, closer to the yawning fissure that had opened in the blast's wake. He crawled toward me, eyes wide.

Gunfire erupted below, and Barthandelus howled, enraged. Another blast tore through the cabin, and the far wall behind us disintegrated, obliterating the space where Vayne had been kept. The loft shuddered forward, its remaining support beams unable to withstand the weight bearing down upon the structure. The floor beneath us tilted. I looked over the edge and found that Barthandelus's top hat had fallen to the floor. When I looked to him, I discovered that a flap of scalp hung loosely over the side of his face, and blood poured from the hole where the bullet had punched a massive hole through his skull. Another round had connected with his left shoulder and elbow as well as his right hand. The shoulder had fared the best from its encounter, but his arm beneath the elbow hung on frayed strands of flesh and

189

dangled uselessly. His right hand was a disfigured stump beyond the wrist.

Jessica hadn't retrieved her Sig Sauer. She'd gone for her Desert Eagle .44 Magnum.

Shots like this would have dropped any ordinary man. Barthandelus, however, wasn't easily put down. He staggered around, roaring, and another blast of scarlet light erupted from his face. Jessica dove over the couch and out of sight as the rays tore through multiple stacks of impossible collectibles and the far end of the couch.

I turned, searching what remained of the loft for my firearm. Six feet beyond my reach, it was lodged between a nightstand and the far wall. When the floor shifted, the nightstand slid against the wall, pinning the gun.

Above, the supports groaned. I didn't have much time. I needed the gun, but I couldn't risk going for it. The shift of weight could be just enough to hasten the destruction of the loft.

I reached a hand toward the gun, closed my eyes, and focused. In my mind's eye, I pictured the Sig Sauer, could almost feel the smooth grip in my hand. I imagined the nightstand sliding aside, then with an extra bit of effort, I exerted a small *push* of thought, and the Sig Sauer slipped into my hand.

One of my newly acquired abilities since the events in Scarborough Hill, I'd discovered, was telekinesis.

I scrambled to my feet and leaped over the edge of the loft as it ripped free and began to fall. I crashed down atop a mound of paperback books (which scattered, ripped, and split beneath me), rolled, and shot to my feet, raising the Sig Sauer as I did so. The loft crashed to the floor behind me.

Vayne had also jumped. As I ran at Barthandelus, readying

myself for a closer shot, he yelled, *"Stop using* my *mana!"*

The figure turned toward Vayne, his head tilting upward, the blast of mana continuing to usher from his countenance as it ripped above the couch and tore through the windows, blasting them out into the cold night beyond. Dancing snowflakes borne on the cold air drifted into the cabin.

I kicked aside a stack of DVDs, pushing through into the next path as I took aim, confident that I was close enough to hit my mark. The gaping hole in the side of Barthandelus's skull was turned away from me, but I could see the side of his face as he turned. Even through the swath of scarlet light, I could see his eyes, and they were focused wholly on Vayne as Barthandelus turned to rain hell down upon him.

I fired once, twice, thrice in quick succession. Each round hit its mark, striking Barthandelus in the side of the head. The first decimated his temple, reducing his eye to a blast of gore in what remained of its orbital socket. The other two struck the side of his head with enough force to punch through and spray the air beyond with blood and brain matter as they exited the open wound.

Barthandelus sunk to one knee, the light of Vayne's consumed mana fading. He turned his head ever so slowly, his one remaining eye fixing me with its stare. Surprisingly, to my horror, it remained very much lucid.

"You are wrong to think I will be put down so easily."

I shot him again, and he collapsed. Whereas in the past I have felt sorrow and regret in committing such violence, now I felt nothing.

I wasn't cold-blooded, but I was a killer nonetheless.

191

I found Jessica behind the couch still, stunned but alive. The blast had come a bit too close for comfort, I discovered, for the tread on the bottom of her shoes had been partially sheared off. The blasts of mana conducted no heat but were concussive, and while they hit objects at the epicenter of the blast with the force of a bomb, anything along the periphery of the blast could still find the mana slicing through it like a knife through butter. The blast had disoriented her but she military crawled toward end of the couch that hadn't been blown to smithereens in an effort to evade Barthandelus's murderous rage.

The three of us – Jessica, Vayne, and I –gathered around the end of the couch, collecting our wits as we cast the occasional glance at our fallen foe. After she saw the damage I'd wrought upon Barthandelus, Jessica took my face in her hands, looked deep into my eyes, and asked if I was alright. I nodded, but I wasn't entirely sure that was the case.

I hadn't been alright for some time.

Vayne sat on the edge of the couch, shaking his head as he studied Barthandelus's body. "It shouldn't have been that easy to put him down," he said, looking back at me and Jessica. "He's a Unatoan. You practically have to banish them from the realm to stop them."

"A una-what?" Jessica asked.

"Unatoan. Walking death. Devourer of souls. That's why he wanted me. He wanted to absorb my mana, then he intended to complete the Ritual of Yuul. It would've increased his power exponentially."

Jessica shot me a look of bafflement. I shook my head. "I'm sorry, I'm hearing too many terms I don't understand. What is the Ritual of Yuul?"

"He would have taken my soul. Normally he doesn't need to conduct a ritual. With magical entities such as Opopanax, however, it's the only way to subdue it."

Jessica and I exchanged a look. "You called him the walking death?" she asked.

Vayne nodded. "A devourer of souls. Don't let his appearance fool you. He may have once been human, but he hasn't been for a long time. He hasn't been what you would call *alive* either. He is the personification of death itself."

My gaze settled on the body. Personification of death itself or not, he certainly *seemed* dead.

"Hello?" a voice called, and we all looked to the door where Ron, the bellhop, had entered the cabin from the door leading back to the Inn. "Is everyone alright?"

"Hardly," the body on the floor growled, *"but you'll fix that."*

Jessica and I raised our guns, aiming them at Barthandelus, but he lifted off the floor with such speed that our bullets buried themselves in the floor. He sailed across the room, his phantasmagoric form dripping gore as he went, and landed on his feet before Ron.

"Yes, you'll do quite nicely."

Barthandelus took Ron's head in his hands and snapped his neck with an audible and horrific *crack!*

"TAKE HIM DOWN!" Jessica bellowed, and opened fire, her Desert Eagle booming with every gunshot. I was firing as well, and the two of us advanced on the bloody figure, disintegrating flesh with every well-placed shot, but he did not go down.

We had crossed half the room when the firearms went dry.

Ron's desiccated corpse dropped to the floor, his pigment drained, his eyes rheumy and vacant. Barthandelus turned, and I watched as the flesh around his head wounds healed rapidly. The obliterated eye-socked reformed, as did the orb within, and soon he regarded us with two perfect eyes brimming with malignant glee as the rest of his mutilated form regained its previous perfection.

He laughed. "Fools! You thought you could end me, Bartholomew Barthandelus? *Please.* Bloody amateurs."

A voice cut through the room then, a new presence none of us had been aware of. "Allow me to try then." Abruptly, a dagger seemed to materialize in Barthandelus's throat, its ornate hilt protruding from torn flesh around a geyser of blood.

Through the blasted windows had come a tall figure in a red, flowing cloak held together in the front by an assortment of red and black sashes. The hilts of crisscrossing swords rose to either side of his head from where they were sheathed against his back. His face, already partially obscured by his hood, was wrapped in belts, sashes, and bandages. His black boots gave voice to sonorous thunderclaps, filling the cabin with their boisterous steps.

I recognized the figure immediately. A painting of him hung above the bed in our room back at the Inn.

Barthandelus reached up. With one deft jerk, he removed the dagger from his throat and snarled. He shouldn't have been able to speak, not with his vocal cords severed, yet he did so anyway. *"You hooded bastard."*

"I've come to take him back," the figure said, casting a glance at Vayne. I saw his eyes, like Vayne's, were red; despite this, I doubted he was like Opopanax. I sensed something about him was different.

"His soul is mine!" Barthandelus snarled, approaching the hooded figure. *"He belongs to me now!"*

Despite the bandages, I could see the figure smirk. "He belongs to no one but himself, to whom he has remained true even in his captivity. You, however, cannot even address yourself by your true name, can you, Enmerkar?"

"THAT NAME AND YOURS HAVE BEEN LOST TO TIME, WARRIOR!" Barthandelus screamed. He spat a mouthful of blood onto a nearby stack of impossible artifacts.

"But I have not been," the figure contested. "I have crossed immemorial time and space to find you and others like you, searching for battles only I can wage. I assure you, your name is Enmerkar, and your fight is not with these people but with me, for I am your equal, sir."

"Then let me rip the tongue from your skull," Barthandelus sighed, "so you'll never speak our names again."

We stood, transfixed, as the two met in a flash, the hooded warrior drawing his ōdachi in swift pulls. As the battle ensued, I caught glimpses of Barthandelus running across the blades, flipping and kicking, punches thrown, and yet the hooded figure evaded most of his attacks and countered. The slashes he intended to land always hit their target, and blood jettisoned along multiple arcs through the air.

Finally, Barthandelus knelt before the warrior, his limbs useless, his body bloody and lacerated, head bowed. He growled then, reminding me of the snarls of a wounded dog. "You'll never kill me."

The hooded warrior sheathed one of his ōdachi. "I do not intend to kill you, but I shall banish you from this realm. Never again will you step beneath its skies."

Barthandelus raised his head. "You'll deny me access to the spaces between? You'll trap me forever in one world, where I'll feed indefinitely on its populace?"

"I'll do more than that," he vowed. "You'll be locked away from the world. You'll see no living thing other than the bugs that share your tomb."

Barthandelus opened his mouth to object, but the warrior slashed at the Unatoan's throat. In one deft movement, he was beheaded, his cranium spinning back through the air.

Next to me, Jessica involuntarily flinched. We had each watched the events unfold in a stupor, unable to act as the encounter unfolded before us. Barthandelus's beheading, however, was so abrupt, it broke through our stupor, and our paralysis was replaced by action. I stepped forward – to do what, I'm not sure – but the warrior's reflexes were far faster than my own. He planted one boot on the Unatoan's chest and, as he leaped forward, drove the body to the floor. I could hear bones crack as they broke under his step, and he snatched the head by the hair before it could hit the ground. He lifted the head, peering into Barthandelus's eyes. The Unatoan's mouth worked, forming words, but no voice issued from his lips.

The warrior spoke once more, and the syllables he uttered were mostly alien to me. *"Unatoan en sevokah de 'merna."*

The disembodied head and the dismembered body both combust into blue flames that quickly turned white, burning so bright and fierce to be nearly blinding, forcing us all to avert our gaze. In seconds, the remains were ash, and the warrior held nothing in his grasp but one of his ōdachi, which he sheathed.

The warrior turned to us. "I trust the three of you are well?"

I nodded. Jessica swallowed. "Yes," she said.

"Good," he said. "I must thank you for coming to Vayne's aid. I fear it took me far longer to track him than it should have."

"Of course," I said. "Anyone would have."

The warrior smirked. "No, not just anyone. Many would have turned and run with their tails tucked." He stepped forward, regarding me with great interest. "I suspect Opopanax reached out to you directly, am I correct?"

The dream. I couldn't say Opopanax reached out to me exactly. Quite the opposite, in fact. I wasn't about to argue with a man with swords longer than my body, however, especially after his most recent display of skill. "Yes."

He smiled. "Thank you for answering the call. I am in your debt. Should I find occasion to repay you, I shall do so."

I nodded, unsure of how to respond.

The warrior turned to Vayne. "Shall we go?"

"We shall." He turned to me and Jessica. "Thank you, both of you. Shall we ever cross paths again, I will find a way to repay you as well."

Vayne stepped to the warrior's side, who nodded to us before turning away. Vayne did the same. A moment later, the warrior spoke in his weird tongue again – *"Portaj en'merna!"* – and a blue, swirling cloud burst forth in empty space. The warrior stepped forward, slipping into it and thus disappearing beyond its veil.

Vayne cast one final look back at us. He nodded. I nodded back. Then he was gone. The portal closed, leaving Jessica and me in the cabin of impossible artifacts.

## NINE

Upon our return to the Inn, Sam the barkeep led several others through the doorway to Barthandelus's cabin. There, they retrieved Ron's remains and brought them back under a shroud.

I asked Sam what they would do with him. "We take care of our own," he said before absconding with the corpse into the bowels of the Inn, down the back corridors where only employees were permitted. CindyLou thanked us for what we had done before she, too, disappeared.

Back in our room, I did not expect to find sleep, but I did… although I don't think I found it so much as it not only found but *tackled* me. My exhaustion was deep and profound, and while others may claim not to have dreamed during such a state, I cannot say the same.

The dream was disturbing to say the least and once again served as a reminder that, even here, in a place far removed from the world at large, the problems I sought to escape still awaited me. I had no illusions I would evade the ominous forces which insisted upon playing antagonist in my story, but I intended to do so for as long as possible. In facing Barthandelus, I acted without hesitation whereas months ago I would have shrunken from such abhorrent violence. I might not have ultimately stopped Barthandelus myself, but had he been human, I would have.

Moving forward, I would not hesitate. I knew that now. I might question who I was as a person, but I was no longer the frail nomad, determined to slip through encounters by the skin of my teeth. I would do what I must to protect those I loved and those who could not protect themselves. If our night at the Inn had done one thing, it had convinced me I could not simply disappear and expect never to be found. Therefore, I would adapt and learn. When the time ultimately came, I would be ready for whatever horrors awaited me.

Upon waking, Jessica and I prepared to depart the Inn. "You don't think we'll have any problem leaving, do you?" she asked.

"No," I replied. "I think we'll walk out those doors and find our car right where we found it."

In the shower, as Jessica applied a soaped-up loofah to my back, thoroughly scrubbing my shoulders and the space between, she said, "You were talking in your sleep."

"Was I?"

"Who's Lindsay?"

The memory of her face was clear, but outside the realm of dreams, I'd never seen her before. Her exotic purple eyes, however, were astonishing and instantly recognizable. "I don't know. She's with Sullivan though. Of that much, I'm sure."

"Sullivan? I thought Black 9 took him."

"They did. I believe he's escaped." I hesitated on my next point. "I saw something else though."

"What?"

"Me."

"You?"

"Yes, me."

I turned, and she painted a swath of suds against my chest. "What do you mean, *you?*"

"I was with Sullivan."

"But you're not with Sullivan."

"I know."

"You're here, with me." She reached back, caught some of the cascading water from the showerhead in her hand, and flung it across my chest.

"I know. I can't make sense of it either."

She smirked. "Who says you make any sense?"

"I'd like to think I at least make a modicum of sense."

She leaned against me, her body tight against mine. "You'd like to think."

"I do like to think."

"What else do you like to do?"

"Plenty."

I kissed her, and then we forgot about *actually* showering for a bit.

TEN

Checkout procedures at the Inn were rather lax. CindyLou thanked us again for what we had done the night before as we handed over our key. "I do hope you'll visit us again," she said as we turned to leave.

The pixie-ish girl from the brothel was standing by the doors, although now she was fully dressed in maître d' attire. She smiled as we approached.

"You know," I said, "I never caught your name last night."

She smirked. "I didn't think you needed it."

"We'd still like to know," Jessica piped up.

"Savannah," she replied. "Now that you know my name, have a pleasant journey. I must be going. I believe Mr. Wallace is awaiting me in the restaurant."

I didn't know who Mr. Wallace was, but I understood her meaning all too clear: *duty calls.*

As she walked away, I turned and surveyed the lobby once more. I sensed what I saw wasn't the Inn as it truly was, that beneath the décor I surveyed was the true face of the Inn. This place, I surmised, was a chameleon. Not quite an illusion, perhaps, but close to it.

"You ready?" Jessica asked.

"Yeah, I think so," I said, and we stepped out into sunlight.

Our car was exactly where we'd left it, but the parking lot was in disrepair whereas it hadn't been the night before. When we turned back to look at the Inn, we discovered an empty lot overgrown with weeds.

Anyone else might have been surprised, maybe even frightened, but not us. We'd seen far worse.

Jessica and I loaded our belongings into the car.

"I'll drive," she said as we were about to close the trunk.

"No, no, I'll drive," I countered.

She produced a coin. "I'll flip you for it."

I nodded.

"Call it," she said, and flipped the coin.

"Tails," I called at the coin's apex.

The coin turned over in the air, somersaulting from heads to tails, tails to heads, sunlight glinting off its surface. Jessica snatched it out of the air, slammed it onto the back of her hand, and revealed the driver.

Acknowledgements

-and-

About the Authors

Thomas A Farmer

About the Author

https://www.facebook.com/tafarmerauthor/
https://www.amazon.com/Thomas-A-Farmer/e/B01A436HFO/

Born to geeky parents and raised on a diet of Star Trek and Babylon 5, Thomas started writing at an early age, managing to keep the hobby alive long enough to make something of it. He's quite glad some of those early drafts and stories no longer exist, though his mother, as mothers do, claims she has copies of them.

Writing occupied much of his spare time throughout school and the years after, eventually culminating in an ostensible *magnum opus* he calls the "Chronicles of St. Michael." To this date, those stories still reek of many "early writer" problems, but he promises they will, one day, see the light of publication.

His first novel, "The Week the World Ended" came to him when a dream about monsters that stole water meshed with the spoken ending of Alice Cooper's "Devil's Food." Another of his upcoming novels, "Scourge of Gods," came to him in a fever dream while recovering from food poisoning. "It's not the best way to get ideas," he says.

When his hands aren't full with books, reading or writing, he fills them with swords. Four nights a week, as of this publication anyway, he teaches historic fencing, also called HEMA (Historic European Martial Arts) as one of the head coaches of the Knoxville Academy of the Blade.

You can find out more about HEMA at https://www.hemaalliance.com/

He lives with his wife, Stephanie, their three cats, lizard, and snake.

Acknowledgements

He'd like to dedicate the anthology itself to his father, John Farmer, who originally gave him the idea, and continue to pester him about it until he did something with it. He would also like to thank Lisa Marie Orta, who provided immense help during the editing process.

Upcoming Works

"The Stars Have Eyes" – Late 2017/early 2018. What happens when you explore too far?

"Scourge of Gods" – 2018. The consequences of hubris are inescapable.

And, of course, "Inn Between Worlds: Volume 2" – 2018, with luck.

Amie Gibbons

About the Author

Amie was born and raised in the Salt Lake Valley. She started making up stories before she could read and would act them out with her dolls and stuffed animals. She started actually writing them down in college, just decided to do it one day and couldn't stop.

She took an unplanned hiatus from writing when she went to Vanderbilt Law School and all of her brain power got consumed by cases, statutes, exams, and partying like only grad students in Nashville can. She graduated and picked her writing back up as soon as her brain limped back in after the bar exam.

She loves urban fantasy and is obsessed with the theory of alternate realities. Whether or not she travels to them in the flesh or just in her mind is up for debate.

She spends her days living the law life and her nights writing when she's not hitting downtown Nashville to check out live music or inflict her singing on the crowds at karaoke bars. She lives with a cat trapped in a man's body, who doesn't complain about being trapped since it allows him the use of opposable thumbs to work his camera, and his best friend, a man trapped in a cat's body, who complains about his lack of opposable thumbs daily.

She has a dozen short stories and four books out, which can be found here: https://www.amazon.com/Amie-Gibbons/e/B01651YIZU. Her most popular series is the SDF paranormal mystery series about spunky psychic Ariana Ryder.

To hear about new releases, sign up for her mailing list here: http://eepurl.com/bzelVv

Acknowledgements

It's never easy to thank everyone who helped with a book, and I'm sure I'll inevitably leave people out; it's not on purpose, I swear.

First up, of course, thank you to my family, but my parents and siblings in particular. Mom, you taught me to love reading. Dad, you were right, never should've taught me how to read, look what happens.

To my first reader, my twin six years removed. Probably shouldn't have subjected you to some of those terrible first tries, but look how well it turned out, baby brother.

And then to all the people who cheered me on during writing, then beta read and edited this book: Sam, my best beta reader. Tiffany, one fantastic editor. And my many wonderful beta readers who helped smooth out the rough spots.

And, as always, thank you to my kitteh. You never think I'm weird or rude, you bring me chocolate and you calm me down, but know when to let me just spaz out.

Michael David Anderson

About the Author

www.michaeldavidanderson.com

https://www.facebook.com/authorMichaelDavidAnderson/

www.twitter.com/shadeofmidnight

Michael David Anderson is the author of the Teddy Dormer novels, Teddy and Wake, and their companion piece Desynchrony. He possesses degrees in both Psychology and English. He was born in East Tennessee in 1985 and currently resides in Knoxville. When asked what type of novels he writes, he is often given looks of utter distaste and downright horror. "That's the look I expected you to give me," he often tells them.

In addition to writing horror and suspense novels, Anderson is a poet, gamer, and stand-up comic. His dogs, Bandit and Rory, serve as a constant distraction from his writing.

Acknowledgements

Tom approached me about the Inn a while back – if memory serves me right, I was still working on my forthcoming novel *In the House of Wolves* at the time – to gauge my interest in writing a story for the anthology. I remember thinking it was an intriguing concept, but I wasn't sure what to write initially. I considered the idea of sending Teddy Dormer, the protagonist of my first two novels *Teddy* and *Wake,* to the Inn, but I didn't know how I'd get him there.

Time passed, and I saw Tom at another event. Once again, the Inn came up. The first draft of *In the House of Wolves* was complete, and I had a little bit of time on my plate to venture into some side work. I decided if I was going to write a Teddy Dormer story involving the Inn, I wanted it to be canon to the other works, and I wanted to explore some of the more intriguing aspects of the

Inn. I also saw it as an opportunity to explore some of the more extraordinary ideas in the mythos I'm creating and pull back the curtain on yet another corner of the multiverse.

For those of you who haven't read my novels, I also wanted to write a story that could be easily consumed without having read 800-plus pages of material that had come before. Here, you get a sliver of Teddy's world, and I've hopefully supplied you with any of the relevant pieces you need. For those of you have read the tales, hopefully this whets your appetite until Teddy shows up again… although when that can be, I can't tell you.

Not yet.

Coming Soon:

"In the House of Wolves" (novel) - 2017

"The Consequences of Wish Fulfillment" - story collected in *Collateral Damage*, a Superhero Anthology edited by Steve Beaulieu - 2017

Short film adaptation of "Inside Out" - 2017

"Black Tie, White Noose" (poetry book) - 2018

www.ingramcontent.com/pod-product-compliance
Lightning Source LLC
Chambersburg PA
CBHW051251250626
47155CB00009B/3258